PARK CITY VOLUME 2

BY

SHAWN GREEN

Also By Shawn Green

Park City Volume One

Revere Street

THE BIGGEST MISTAKE ANY NIGGA EVER MAKE IS GETTING TOO COMFORTABLE. KICKING THEIR FEET UP. TAKING THAT MOTHERFUCKING VICTORY LAP. CUZ YOU AIN'T NEVER SAFE. SOMEBODY ALWAYS OUT THERE WATCHING. AND BY THE TIME YOU SEE EM IT'S ALREADY TOO LATE.

Curtis fifty cent Jackson.

THE WHISPER OF DEATH

PROLOGUE

Joe Dickerson and his lawyer Michael Vintoro sat in the conference room of Michael's Law firm. Which is located in the heart of Stamford Connecticut. The conference room was big and spacious. With a huge round table in the center of the room. It also has pictures of past governors of Connecticut. Also, past mayors of Stanford. In all of the pictures it has Michael and Joe in them. The conference room also has a nice view of downtown Stamford. Joe looks out the window while drinking his morning coffee. Looking at the different stores and restaurant. Like Dunkin' Donuts, Bobby V's just to name a few. Listening to what Michael has to say concerning his lawsuit against the city of Bridgeport, and the Bridgeport police department. It has been a year and a half. Since he was released from prison. Because of the corruption in the forensic lab. "The city of Bridgeport, and the police department. Decided to settle out of court." Says Michael while staring at Joe. Michael repeated himself again to make sure Joe heard him. Because Joe looked like he was in a trance or daydreaming. "You don't have to repeat yourself I heard you. I just have a lot on my mind."

Michael stands up from the conference table and walk towards Joe. Wondering what is wrong with him. Michael starts to feel concerned for him. "What's on your mind? You can tell me Joe. I am much more than your lawyer I am your friend." Joe continues to stare out of the window. Looking down at downtown Stamford. Watching people going about their daily life. "Me and you been friends since grade school." Says Joe Dickerson in a compassions tone. "You know how I was raised. How I came up. What it took for me to get here." "I know Joe. You crawled out of the projects to get." Michael says with some conviction. "I am not going to let some piece of shit cop take everything away from me. Or my family." "Are you talking about detective Hagen?"

Michael Says with some concern. Joe shakes his head yes. "Detective Hagen is good at playing politics. His time as the head of Bridgeport police cold case unit, and at 911 operation. He was able to learn and gather dirt on a lot of powerful people. That is what saved him." Joe

Dickerson turns to Michael and speaks. "I do not tolerate people going after my family." Joe Says with such anger and hatred. Slamming his coffee on the conference table. Making a mess on the table and floor. Michael grabs him by the shoulder to calm him down. Joe begins to relax. Michael call for a janitor to clean up the mess. "The mayor tried to get detective Hagen fired with no success. Plus, the new police chief is going to be a problem. He is former head of internal affairs." Joe looks at Michael with a surprise look on his face. Like a person who can't believe what just happened. "Gill Ridges is the new chief. How in the hell did that happen?" Michael threw both of his hands up then says. "I don't know. The mayor is not commenting." Call your father and our guy in Long Island. I believe Bridgeport needs a new mayor." "Done I will make the call." Before he leaves to make the call. He stops at the conference room door. He turns to look at Joe Dickerson. Who is still looking out of the window.

Michael begins to contemplate on weather to discuss another matter to him. Which concerns his brother. He was made aware that not only the Italians, but everyone else in Dickerson's organization wants his brother dead. He decides to leave it alone. He then leaves to his office to make the calls.

CHAPTER ONE

Detective Green pulls up to Whites Diner on Boston Avenue. He sees detective Hagen already there sitting talking to a Police officer in his class a uniform. He appears to have Captains bars on his uniform. He starts to wonder what is going on. A lot of things are starting to race threw his mind. He had heard of Detective Hagen. Getting his badge back. The brief time he knew him he felt that he was a good detective. Also, many other police officers were either fired our suspended because of the Attorney General's investigation into the Bridgeport Police Department. Which was a result of the death of the mayor of Westport son. Plus, information that detective Hagen had on a lot of police officers. Both Hagen and the mayor of Westport got their revenge. He gets out of the car looks at the clock on the diner. He tells himself that he will order breakfast since he never ate when he got up this morning. Plus, it is only eleven o'clock am still time for breakfast. He walks in the diner a waitress walks up to him. He looks at the waitress up and down a middle age Hispanic women black hair with an average body. He points to the table with Hagen and the unknown Police Captain.

The diner is pretty pack with people. Some eating lunch and some still eating breakfast. He sees pictures of famous people on the wall of the diner. Some are at a table eating some are at the counter eating and watching TV. He seats himself next to Detective Hagen who is drinking a cup of coffee. He greets Hagen then he shakes the hand of captain Martinez. Detective Green sees captain Martinez hands detective Hagen his badge. "You have your job back detective. All charges are dropped." Hagen has a smile on his face. While detective Green stairs at captain Martinez angrily.

The waitress came and offered coffee to the gentlemen. She poured coffee in all their cups then she took detective Green's food order then she left for the kitchen. Hagan look at captain Martinez who was sitting across from him. Then Hagan began to say. "I am leaving" Detective Green gets up to let detective Hagen leave. Once Hagen leaves. Green sit back down and looks at Martinez. "You gave that fuck his job back?" Detective Green Says so loud. "Especially after what that son of a bitch did to me." Continues detective Green. Martinez tries to calm detective Green. Then a hand grabs detective Green on the shoulder. Green turns to his left to see who grabs him.

He recognized the person as Bridgeport fire chief Zigway. Green calms himself down and Zigway sits himself down next to detective Green. "Don't blame captain Martinez for Hagen getting his job back." Zigway Says while looking detective Green in the eye. Detective Green remains calm while staring at fire chief Zigway in his class a firefighter uniform. "Hagen played the political game to get his job back. He had dirt on everyone in the Bridgeport police department. From his days in the cold case unit and 911 operation." Green starts to laugh like someone said something funny.

Martinez takes a sip of coffee. Then says. "The reason I asked you hear detective Green is because. I want you to partner up with Hagen." After Martinez Says that detective Green slams his coffee cup on the table. Which causes everyone to stare at them again. Fire chief Zigway grabs Green to calm him down. Zigway yells at Martinez to come back and sit down. Martinez comes back cautiously to the table and sits down. The waitress comes to their table. With a look that reminds detective Green of his mother. The same look she would give him when she is angry. "I don't care if you guys are police officers and firefighters.

One more disruption like that again. You will be removed from the premises." After she says that. She cleans up the broken glass. Then she gives detective Green another up of coffee. Then goes back to other customers. Detective Green looks at Martinez with so much hatred and anger. "You want me to work with a guy. That illegally investigated me. Plus release my family information to everyone. Ruining my promotion, and the job I had with the FBI." Chief Zigway pats detective Green on the shoulder. Trying to calm him down. With much success.

Captain Martinez then begins to say. "I truly understand detective. I know you lost your promotion to lieutenant, but hear is your Sargent's badge" Captain Martinez hands detective Green his Sargent's badge. "Our new Chief wants you to have a partner." Before Martinez can continue Green cuts him off by saying. "Fuck the chief. He is just mad that I am out doing his hand pick detective. Plus the press is starting to ask questions about the way I am treated." Martinez is starting to look frustrated. He begins to shake is head sideways then says at the same time. "I cannot with this guy. You talk to him Zigway." Martinez then gets up and leave. Chief Zigway then sits across from detective Green.

Zigway takes a sip of coffee then says. "In a way I don't blame you for acting the way you did." Detective Green starts to feel some relief. That his stepfather agrees with him. "They had no right asking that of you. Especially after what Hagen did to you and me. Mainly you. Don't worry I am going to talk to the new chief of police." Detective Green displays a smirk look on his face. He doesn't like the new chief of police. Which are Gill Ridges former head of Internal Affaires. Tried to have detective Green arrested but couldn't do to lack of evidence. Plus, detective Hagen gave the press information on corrupt police officers, and politicians in the city of Bridgeport. He collected all that information during his time as a cold case investigator, and a 911 operator.

"You know I don't like that guy. He tried to have me arrested on trumped up charges. He also cost me my new job and promotion. I should be a lieutenant now. Not a sergeant." Says detective Green with so much anger. Everyone turned to look at them again. The waitress starts to come back to their table. Zigway gets up and cuts her off and begins talking to her. Zigway then comes back to the table then says. "You have to control your anger. Because if you don't it will get you into trouble. That is what chief Ridges wants" Detective Green agrees with Zigway. While he sips his coffee.

"Ridges is on a crusade. To clean up this city and police department." Detective Green continues to agree with the fire chief. "Especially after what happened to his family." "I know what he went through. But that don't give him the right to judge me. The way he did just because my brother is the city's biggest drug dealer." Says detective Green. "I heard you turned down two million dollars?" Zigway asked while leaning back in the chair. Giving detective Green a sadistic grin. Detective Green laughs then says. "Yes I did turn it down. I don't want nothing from my family. I don't care if it's legal our illegal." Zigway shakes his head in discuss. "You are the dumbest black person I know. That money was part of a lawsuit your family won. You have every right to that money. I accepted it on your behalf. I put it in the bank under your original last name Dickerson." Detective Green slams his hands on the table. The looks at fire chief Zigway with so much hatred.

They both hear a person yells "excuse me gentleman?" They see a Bridgeport police officer with sergeant bars on his uniform. White police officer. Both Green and Zigway knows him as sergeant Garcia. "Detective Green you are needed at Bridgeport university. We have a serious situation at the moment. The school his now on lock down." Detective Green gets up and runs to his car.

CHAPTER TWO

TWO HOURES EARLIER

Amber Willcots wakes up in her boyfriend's dorm room. He is still asleep next to her. She turns to look at the clock on his dresser. A Dallas Cowboy clock she got for him for Christmas on the NFL store. It reads 9:00am she gets up and looks at her class schedule. She has advance Biology at 10:30am. She gets out of bed looking for her t shirt and panties. Her head still hurts from last night. Her and her boyfriend went out last night. They went to Murphy's Law last night an Irish bar. It was college night last night. She stands up from off the bed. Still feeling a little woozy from all the alcohol, she drinks last night. Amber looks again at the schedule she begins to remember that she has a test in Advanced Biology. She starts to get mad at herself for not studying.

Amber walks to the dresser she picks some clothes she has in his dorm room. She keeps some clothes here just in case she spends the night. Last night was one of those nights. Amber grabs blue Jeanes, white socks, and a white t shirt along with her boyfriend's New York Yankee's jersey. She takes a shower dry's herself off with a towel in the bathroom. Put the clothes on then some perfume on. She kisses him on the cheek. He moves a little but not waking up. Grabs her book bag then walks out of the dorm room. There are lot of people coming and going. Some of the guys have no shirts on and only towels on as pants. She got on the elevator there were some people on it. All of them wearing shorts and shirts and saying, "How hot it is outside" She is thinking to herself that maybe she shouldn't have put on the Yankee Jersey. Amber takes the elevator from the sixth floor to the first floor.

She finds her roommate sitting in the main hallway waiting for her. She is having on some blue sweatpants and a University of Bridgeport T shirt on. She gets up off of the couch and begins to walk towards Amber. They give each other a hug and begin to walk outside. Before they go outside her roommate says to her. "Advance Biology was cancelled." Amber looks at her surprisingly. "Are you serious? Don't be fucking with me? I can use the extra day." Smiling while saying that. They walk outside and see a lot of people outside. Some are laying on the grass just having casual conversation. Some are playing ultimate Frisbee. Some on the far end are playing soccer. A lot of food venders are out. Some are playing music and dancing. It's a beautiful day Amber thought she sees a lot of people heading to the beach.

That is the one thing she likes about this collage is that it is located at Seaside Park. Which is a beautiful park and has a beach. On a nice day like this it makes this collage one of the best. "When is your next class? Mine is at two o'clock pm." Amber tells her roommate. Her roommate opens her book bag checks her schedule. "Same here let's go to the cafeteria get some food then hang out in the Quad." They both walk toward the cafeteria which is on the other side of the college. They get to the library where there are people passing out flyers. They walk up to the group which is all women screaming. "No means no" Very loudly with their fist in the air. A crowd gathers around the group. Amber and her roommate stand in the middle and watches. While Amber watches she feels a quick stinging feeling on her neck. Then a voice that says. "May God have mercy on your soul because I don't." Amber collapsed to the ground. Her roommate dropped to the ground trying to find out what happened to Amber. She screams for help very loudly. While the crowd around her do the same thing.

The killer escape through the confusion without being seen. Continue to walk slowly towards the direction where Amber and her roommate came from. Then the killer disappears in the dorms while a lot of students where running in the dormitory.

CHAPTER 3

PRESENT TIME

Detective Green pull up to the crime scene. Part of lower Park Avenue is blocked off. From Famous pizza on down. A large crowd gathered in front of Famous Pizza. Detective Green can see the owner selling personal pizza in front of the restaurant. Trying to cash in on the large crowd. He see police officers everywhere along with swat teams. There are reporters everywhere news 12, channel eight. Are the ones he notice. The others he don't. Detective Green turns the car off and grabs the door handle. He left the car and started to walk were the crime scene tape is. He get ambushed by a sea of reporters. Asking him questions putting cameras in his face. He cross the crime scene tape. He is met by a police officer in regular uniform with sergeant's bars on. Detective Green knows him as Jack Olestra. A typical white average cop. Plus, captain Martinez was there to.

Along with the medical examiner and the CSI tech. Detective Green look and see the swat teams packing up their gear and leaving. He started to walk toward the CSI tech and the medical examiner. Then captain Martinez grabs Greens shoulder. Detective Green stops looks at the captain and speaks. "Why did you stop me?" "I meant what I said back at the diner. You need a partner. If not Hagan, then someone else. That is a direct order." Martinez saying that with such fierce. So that everyone heard him. Detective Green shrugs it off. Saying to himself. "Martinez just wanted to look good in front of the cameras." Detective Green continues to walk towards the medical examiner. Leaving captain Martinez by himself. Detective Green passes other police officers who were getting statements from people. Some were crying. Some still have the look of shock on their face.

He finally caught up with Dr. Chen. Head of the medical examiner department. He is wearing his typical uniform. The dark blue coat that says medical examiner on it. He is bent down examining the victim. "Just to think. You turned down the position of head of medicine in a hospital in Hong Kong. For a job in this shit hole of a city." Says detective Green with a smile on his face. "Yes, that is true detective. I turned down that job so my daughter can go to school here in America." Detective Green starts to feel bad about the comment he made. "I am sorry. I was just busting your balls." "Don't worry about it detective. At least I know you still have a sense of humor." Dr. Chen gave Green a reassuring smile. That made Green feel good. "Word of advice detective. Your Lone Ranger police work has made other police officers look so badly lately."

"That's why captain Martinez wants me to have a partner so bad." "Yes and no." Detective Green starts to feel both confused and curious. "Crime is on the rise in Bridgeport. All the good detectives got either forced retirement or arrested. Thanks to detective Hagen. Our new chief may disband the narcotic team just to have good detective on the street. You are the only detective closing cases." "That's very interesting but it still doesn't answer the question. Why they want me to partner up with Hagen?" "He has been labeled a rat. Plus, they found a live grenade on his doorstep." Detective Green starts to feel a little sorry for detective Hagen. He then turns to Dr. Chen and says, "So how did the victim die?"

"That I don't know. Till I get her on the table." Says Dr. Chen while he is examining the body. Detective Green bends down and looks at the victim more closely. He is looking at her with a sense of similarities. Dr. Chen notices the look on Green's face. "Do you know her?" "I have this feeling I know her from somewhere. I just can't put my finger on it. What's her name?" "I don't know. The forensic officer who does know is busy giving the information to chief Ridges." Dr. Chen points to where the chief is being briefed. He is surrounded by police officers in suits. He sees Chief Ridges in his class A police uniform. Detective Green looks at him with so much hatred. He wishes he could transfer out of Bridgeport. The chief will not let him leave. Plus because of the attorney general's investigation into the police department. Which have gotten a lot of police officers arrested or forced to retire. The chief used that to block his transfer to the FBI. Because there weren't enough detectives because of detective Hagen. Revealing that he is the brother of a known criminal. He lost his promotion to Lieutenant also. A person tapped him on the shoulder. He then turns around and sees that it's Sergeant Olestra.

"For the record. Everyone one in the police department has your back. It's not your fault who you are related to." Detective Green starts to feel good inside. He begins to feel he can let up his defenses. "On the other hand. You should've taken that dam money. Criminal brother or not. You have to be the dumbest black person I ever know." The Sargent says with a smile on his face. Green pats him on the back. "Now let's get to business Sargent." Detective Green says. "You can at least buy a better suit. You look like Colombo from the tv show. But you are the black version." "Yeah whatever" they both started laughing at each other.

"The victim is a white female. She is 5'9"and her name is Amber Willcots." Detective Green grabs the shoulder of the sergeant. Dr. Chen gets up and looks at Green. With disbelief and with a shocking look. Sergeant Olestra looks at both with a bewildered look then says. "What's wrong with you both. Y'all have the same look the chief had when I read her name to her." "She is the daughter of the corrupt district attorney. That lieutenant Post arrested five years ago." Green says. "I remember that. That happened before I transferred her to Bridgeport. I also remember they couldn't get him to flip on your brother." Both Green and Chen agreed with Olestra. "Continue sergeant." "The chief made a call to the Warden at Cheshire to notify the father. We have officers talking to her boyfriend. His name is Derek Turner. His uncle is Bruce Turner a detective in New Haven."

"Was you able to get the tapes from the video camera." Detective Green says while pointing to the cameras in the area. "One of the officer's is with captain Martinez now getting them." "Let's get this body out of here once Dr Chen is done. I am off to question the boyfriend." Green leaves Chen and the Sargeant at the crime scene. While walking to the student dormitories. He is met by Lieutenant Post. Who is still in swat gear. He looks like he aged a little. Detective Green knows that Post has been going through a lot lately. His unit may get disbanded. Which will cause him to get reassign. The man under his command is wondering about their future. "You need a vacation. I can tell you are going through a lot." "I just want to say for the record." Both Green and Post stop walking. "You have everyone in this department respect. Except for the chief."

"That fucker will never like me." "Stay away from Hagan. Trust me. Don't partner up with that rat bastard." Post taps Green on the shoulder and walks away. Detective Green continues to the dormitory. Where he is met by captain Martinez. He has a worried look on his face. Detective Green feels happy he is not in Martinez shoes. A dead high profile victim, and a high profile boyfriend. Green doesn't know Detective Bruce Turner. He has heard of him. Excellent missing person detective, he ran the best missing person unit in the state. He even put the F.B.I to shame. "I already questioned the boyfriend. The last time he saw her was when she left for class this morning. They went to Murphy's law last night. It was college night there. The place was packed with college students.

From there they went to his dormitory." "Murphy's law has cameras I will go and retrieve the tapes. I know the bartender and owner well." Martinez agreed with Green. As detective Green walks away from captain Martinez. The captain screams out. "You are going to have a partner weather you like it our not." Green ignores him and continues walking away. As he is walking, he is met by sergeant Olestra. "We will continue to canvass the area. Talk to everyone that is down here." "I want the security tapes brought to my desk at HQ. Do you have the address to Amber mother's house?" Olestra fumbles through his notes. Looking for the address. Detective Green can remember doing the same thing. When he was a patrol officer.

He finally found it. She lives on 132 A Karen court." "I know the area. Thanks sergeant." Detective Green leaves him and continues to walk to the car. Where he is met by chief Ridges. Who is given him a stern sharp look. Green approaches him and stares in his face. Like one of those prize fighters getting ready to fight. "You will take Hagan as your partner. This is a direct order." Says Ridges as spit flies from his mouth. "The only reason why you want me to partner with. That rat bastard is because no one wants him. Plus, everyone in this department wants to kill him for squealing to the attorney general." Chief Ridges balls his fists like he is ready to punch detective Green in the face. Chief Ridges is filled with a lot of emotions. His hatred for Green is swelling right now. He pulls back his arm like he is getting ready to punch detective Green. When a arm grabs him and shove him out the way. "People are filming you two right now." Captain Martinez points to the reporter's and civilians filming with the phones. Chief Ridges walks away.

CHAPTER 4

Jackson pulls into Trumball Avenue from the Reservoir Avenue side. He just finished making the monthly money pickups. He checks his watch then realized it's only twelve pm. He finished early than expected. Mainly because the crew on the south end. Said they will know longer pay anything until Mr. Dickerson renegotiate. The crew on the south side lost part of Marina projects. They have been sold to the university of Bridgeport. The crew on the south side lost about two hundred thousand dollars a week. That's how much they were making at Marina project. From drugs, prostitution, gambling and extorting the businesses in the area. Jackson parks the car in the lot of building number 14. There are only two buildings left on Trumball Avenue.

There's was several of them. Until the city thought it would be a good idea to knock them all down except for two. Then make the rest town houses. Thinking that would cut down on crime in the area. Jackson sits in the car thinking of something to say to David Buckshot. He knows he will be angry about the money being short. His hands begin to shake, and he starts to sweat. He tries to control himself. When a sudden bang on the driver side window scares him so much. He pulls out his Beretta. "Calm down. Calm down. It's just me me." He begins to recognize the man at his window with his hands up.

It's Tony. Everyone calls him T for short. A average looking light skin man. He runs errands for David. Plus, other things which he and David keep secret. Jackson puts the gun away and roll down the window. "What the hell is wrong with you? You are safe, this is our Territory." Tony says. Tony begins to look at Jackson with a concern look. Like he knows something is wrong. He bends down even closer and puts his head in the car. "What the fuck happen?" Tony says in a angry tone. "Those Marina cats said they ain't paying shit. To us anymore. They want a meeting with Mr. Dickerson. To renegotiate everything. Since they took a hit with parts of Marina village was knocked down."

After Jackson finished. Tony started screaming fuck over and over again. He is also pacing back and forth. "Get out of the car and let's go tell David." They both walk into building 14. They get on the only working elevator they press the button for the tenth floor. They make their way to the tenth floor. We're they are met by a group of armed men. With automatic weapons. Tony talks to the leader of the group. Jackson knows him very well. He is a strong black man with a military background. He was discharged from the United States military. He couldn't find a job nowhere. So, Mr. Dickerson gave him a job. Ever since Mr. Dickerson got out of prison, he has been recruiting a lot of X military. The leader of the group came close Tony. "From now on. I am coming with you on the money pick up. All of them." He says with so much conviction. While holding the automatic weapon so tightly. Tony and Jackson walked through a steel door. Which opened led them in a huge room. It looks like it used to be a three-bedroom apartment.

They converted it into a huge cash room with at least ten females counting Money. On a huge, long table wish cash machine. Then there's more men with automatic weapons in the room. They walked to the end of the room to another door. Jackson bangs on the door. Then yells. "It's me Jackson we have a problem." The door opens up. David is sitting behind a desk. Sporting his Yankees jersey with a gold Rolex watch on its right hand. Across from him is an unknown Hispanic male with lots of tattoos. The one tattoo on his neck says MS13. Tony nor Jackson has ever seen him before. The unknown male shakes David's hand then is escorted out. Tony and Jackson sit down in front of David then Tony begins to tell David the problem.

David begins to shake his head. Then he says. "I told him this was going to happen. Once I found out that they sold Marina Village. To the University of Bridgeport." He begins to laugh while he drinks his shot of Hennessy. "Jackson makes sure Tony has protection on all money pickups for now on." "Already taken care of. Your uncles' man in the hallway is on it." Says Jackson. David Smiles from ear to ear. Jackson continues saying. "I believe we should change location of this place. Case they get the balls to attack." David shakes his head in agreement. "Do you have a new location in mind?" David asked. Jackson shakes his head yes. Then a bang came at the door with someone screaming. David opens the door we have a serious problem. Open the door now!" The person screams out. Which makes David, Tony, and Jackson scared.

Tony opens the the door. When they open the door David recognizes the person. Everyone puts their guns away. The guy is exhausted and dripping in sweat. "Catch your breath." The guy started to calm down. Then he begins saying. "Amber Willcots is dead. Someone murdered her." David has a shocking look on his face. He begins to feel scared. He knows Amber's death will lead to big problems. Not only for him but for everyone. "Tony gets the car started." He gets up and leaves to start the car. "If you are going to speak to your uncle directly. I don't think he is back from Long Island." David slams his hands on the desk. Like a person who forgot something. "Then we go to the ferry and wait for him." "With the money we suppose to give. He is not going to like this." Jackson says with a concern look on his face. "Don't be afraid. After we tell him what just happened. He will calm down." They both get up. With Jackson grabbing the money. They head to the car. Once they got in the car. Jackson says to Tony. "Drive to the boss's office."

CHAPTER 5

Detective Green pulls into Karen Court. Which is part of the Stone Ridge Condominiums. He drives all the way to the end of the street. He gets out of the car and enjoys the scenery. This part of Stone Ridge has a lot of trees. There is a very dense forest here. He begins to contemplate on how he was going to give the news to Ms Willcots. That her daughter is dead. This part of the job detective Mike Green hates. "What are you waiting for detective?" Green turns and looks to see who said that. He see's Lieutenant Post. He starts to feel happy that Post is here. He walks to him and shakes his hand. Post is in his class a uniform.

"What are you doing here?" Green asked "one I thought you might need help. Two I figured I might be able to use the situation to get some information. On your brother. Maybe able to convince her to tell her husband to cooperate." Green nods his head in approval. "You might not have too much longer. I heard they may break up your unit." Post makes and angry expression after what Green said. "I have been fighting that for months. The Chief says he needs more detective on the street. We are short detective's and patrol officers. Because of that rat Hagen. Now let's go talk to Ms. Willcots.

They continue to the last condo. On the street. Detective Michael Green. Knocks on the door. He knocks again. Then he hears someone yelling. "Hold on hold on. I am coming. Jesus Christ holds the hell on." The way she said it made detective Green think about his grandmother. She used to say the same thing. When someone is knocking on her door. The door opens and a beautiful blonde, white women open the door. She reminds both officers of Vanna White from wheel of fortune. "Hello, Ms Willcots, I am detective Green, and this is lieutenant Post." Detective Green flashing his badge.

"I know who you are. You are Detective Green. You have been on tv a lot lately. Your related to Joe Dickerson." She gave both men scolding looks. "Are you here on the behalf of the police department, or Joe Dickerson?" "Now what would make you say that?" Says lieutenant Post. Curiously. She begins to look nervous. Now realizing she said something she shouldn't have. She starts to stutter Her words. Then she finally was able to say. "What are you doing here?" "It's very difficult to say. I think we better sit down." "Lieutenant Post I will not let you in my house. Not without a warrant." "Okay. Your daughter is dead." Detective Green says. Ms Willcots begins to cry. She keeps saying. "No no no." Her body begins to shake. After Green shows her the pictures. Lieutenant Post catches her in his arms before she falls. Post escorts her to the couch. She continues to cry nonstop for about two hours. She finally calms down when detective Green asks. "Can we ask you some questions?"

Ms Willcots nods her head yes. With tears coming down her eyes. "Does your daughter have any enemies? Or have you received any death threats?" Lieutenant Post ask her while he has his arms around her in comfort. While the lieutenant is asking her questions. Detective Green begins walking around the condo. He walks up stairs to the second floor. The stairs located in front of the door. He automatically locates Amber's room. First room on the left next to the stairs. He see's a lot of Justin Bieber posters. On the wall. The bed is perfectly made. It has the look like no ones been in it for awhile. Detective Green heads towards the dresser. Where he sees several pictures. Mostly of her and her boyfriend. The one that caught his eye is a picture of Amber and four other girls.

All of which detective Green knows. Especially the Hispanic girl which is Joe's girlfriend's niece. Green grabs the picture and takes it out of the picture frame. He puts it in his pocket. He noticed a diary on the dresser but paid it no mind because it's having a lock on it, and he doesn't have the key. He hears the lieutenant call his name. So, he heads back downstairs. He asks Ms Willcots. "Does your daughter write in her diary a lot?" "Well yes. Come to think about it I was going to bring it to her this weekend. She had lost it, but I found it in my car yesterday. She has the key in her dorm room." Detective Green contemplates Going back upstairs for the diary. Then he decided not to. The lieutenant hands her his card and they both leave.

They make their walk back to the car. Once in the car detective Green shows. Lieutenant Post the picture. His glows like a person who is shocked at what he is seeing. "Everyone in this picture is related to someone in your brother's Organization. Except for this one. The white girl. That is representative Mathew's daughter. He represents Bridgeport in Hartford." Post still has the same expression on his face when he hands Green the photo back. "If he controls the representative of Bridgeport. Then he controls the mayor's office, and who becomes mayor." Detective Green says. "The election is next year. We are in September now. Either this year or next year you are going to lose your unit." After Green finishes what he said. You can see the sad expression on lieutenant Post face. He made his career of of the narcotics team. He and his men have taken down a lot of famous crime organizations. That sprung up in Bridgeport. Joe's organization is the most difficult. Because he is smarter and more careful. Plus, now he knows he has been spreading his money around.

"Continue with your investigation. Leave out the photo for now. Plus, what we learned. We don't know who in the department we can trust. Plus, I need you to find this killer before your brother does." Post says with sadness in his voice.

CHAPTER 6

Joe stairs at the scenery of all the beautiful. Mansions on private island. On the Long Island sound. While standing on the top deck of the Port Jefferson Ferry. He is enjoying the beautiful breeze also on this cool evening. He is happy with the success of the meeting he had. In Long Island. He begins to sense someone behind him. Joe has begun to learn to trust his instincts more. Thanks to recent events. He turns around to see that the person behind him is his long-time friend. Fredric Anderson. You still seam unhappy about wearing a suit. A nice one at that. All black with a white shirt and a nice gold watch on his right hand.

Fredric steps closer to him and is now on his left side. "What's troubling you? You should be happy the way things turned out at the meeting." Fredric says with some concern in his voice. "Just thinking that's all. It's been a bit too quiet lately." Fredric looks at Joe with a look like someone has when they don't understand something you said. "I can tell by the look on your face. You don't know what I am talking about. Me suing the city of Bridgeport, and the Bridgeport Police department. Is nothing.

Since the incident that caused the lawsuit. It's been quiet. Like a calm before the storm." "You must want shit to happen?" "I don't. I am just trying to be one step ahead." Fredric nods his head in approval. "Now tell me this. What are you going to do about your brother?" Joe turns his head towards Fredric. Joe's whole demeanor changes. Then he says with such anger. "What the fuck do you mean? I made it perfectly clear. No one is to harm my brother." Joe said it so loud everyone on the top deck heard them. Michael Vintoro rushed towards Joe to calm him down.

He puts his hands on his shoulder. Joe's starts to relax. Then Michael says. "He is right. Even though the council says your brother will not be harmed. It's the other lower ranked people that you will happen?" "She was at her boyfriends house all night. We thought she was safe. She been spending a lot of time there." Gonzalez turns to David then says. "Don't worry I will contact her father. I will let him know we have nothing to do with this." David nods in agreement. "The Bridgeport Police department put my uncle on the case." "That's perfect I will tell him that. That should ease him a little." "My uncle said meet him at the barbershop downtown. You know which one." Gonzalez nods yes. David leaves and heads back to the car. Once in the car. Tony says. "Is everything okay?" Both Tony and Jackson are concerned because this could turn into a war. Fast if things don't calm down. David nods his head yes. Both Tony and Jackson breathe a side of relief.

Then several men run up to Mr Gonzalez. David recognizes the men. They are Gonzalez foot soldiers. All expert killers. Gonzalez looks at David with a look so fierce. David says immediately. "Drive now. Get he'll out of here." But it was too late. They were already surrounded by Gonzalez men. All of them have their gun out. David, Tony, and Jackson were pulled out of the car. Gonzalez walks up to them then says. "You shut down all my business. Then you don't have the respect to tell me straight out. Giving me false sense of hope that we can solve this peacefully. Now I am going to hold you three hostages till I get what I want." They get taken away while Gonzalez and his bodyguards drive David's car to Joe's Barbershop.

CHAPTER 8

Gonzalez and his bodyguards pull up to the barbershop on Stratford Avenue. It used to belong to someone else. A very close friend of Joe. Joe bought the place from and helped him buy a place in Florida to retire. Gonzalez exists the car along with his bodyguards. He has three of them with him. Before he can get to the entrance of the barbershop. He is met by Joe and his bodyguards. "What the hell are you doing driving my nephew's car?" Gonzalez begins to say with a smile on his face. Like a person who believes he has the upper hand. "I am holding your son hostage. Until you un shut down my business. Plus, we no longer pay you money to operate in Bridgeport. I know you had something to do with the selling of Marina Village. I have people inside city hall to."

Joe begins to tense up with anger. Then his phone begins to ring. He answered it. While at the same time Gonzalez felt disrespected. Because Joe answered the phone. "Your nephew and his boys got kidnapped. I am looking at where they are being held." Joe begins to smile. Again, his boy Fredric came through. "Handle it and call me back when it's done." "I will call you when I have him." Joe hangs up the phone. Then says to Gonzalez. "You made two mistakes. One you put your hands on my family. Then two have the balls to come here in my presence without a army with you. Take his ass." Immediately all of Joe's bodyguards grabs Gonzalez and his men. Plus, more men came out of the barbershop.

Joe received another call. Joe puts the call on speaker. "I have your nephew and we have one hostage. Gonzalez's son. What do you want me to do with him?" Gonzalez begins to get real violent It was hard for the men to hold him. "I am evil but not that evil. Bring him to me alive at the Butcher shop." Joe hangs up the phone. Then says to Gonzalez we're going to the butcher shop." They put him in the car and begin to drive to the butcher shop. "You don't have to do this Joe. We are like family." Gonzalez is saying with an emotional tone. "I just had a new born baby. Who is going to raise her." Gonzalez pleading his case for another five minutes.

When they arrived at the butcher shop. Joe says. "You shouldn't have touched my family. Plus, I know about your business in Waterbury." Gonzalez was shocked by what he said. They reached the back entrance of the butcher shop. We're a white male who is muscular and looks like the Italian version of the Rock. Opens the door then says everything is set up. They led Gonzalez and his three bodyguards to the kitchen. We're Gonzalez son is crying in tears. David is next to him supporting a black eye. Joe walks up to Gonzalez son then says. "Your fathers' territory is mine now. You will work for me. You will report to my nephew David." David smiling after hearing what is uncle said.

"You cross me this is what will happened to you." The muscular man grabs Gonzalez with no problems. While on of Joe's men turned on the machine that is used to grind up meat. He throws Gonzalez in the machine and then there is a loud scream. With Gonzalez son crying out for his father. Joe grabs him while Gonzalez is screaming. Then says. "You cross me this will be you, your mother and your whole family." He nods like he understands. Then Joe says. "Grind the rest of them and put them with the ground meat that is going to the soup kitchen." Joe, Fredric, and David leave the butcher shop. Joe tells his bodyguards to take David to his personal doctor.

They leave in David's car. Joe gets in the car with Fredric then. "Don't worry I got the word out to Mr Willcots. He says he will remain silent as long as you're brother is on the case. If you don't mind me being frank? Why did you give your nephew Gonzalez's territory?" "I want to test his loyalty. You know how close he was with the whole family. Continue to keep an eye on him." He shakes his head yes. Then says. "I am hungry let's go get something to eat."

CHAPTER 9

Detective Michael Green sat at his desk typing the summary of what happened today. Green been sitting at his desk for about an hour doing paperwork. He keeps reminding him self that he would go to Murphy's Law to check it out for himself. Out of know where someone grabs him from behind. Turns to see who it is. it's officer Ashley. Detective Green has been seeing Ashley for about a year and a half. Long black hair. A a beautiful body. That's before she got pregnant. Detective Green stands up and gives her a hug and a kiss. "What time are you coming home tonight?" Ashley asks. "I have to go to Murphy's law and look at some Security tapes. I will be late." She kisses him then leaves. Giving him a sexy smile. Then he sees lieutenant Post walking past her. He screams out to Green. "Meet me in captain Martínez Office."

Green gets up and heads to the office. There has not been that many homicide detective in Bridgeport anymore. Because of the fear of the budget cuts. Also because of detective Hagen. Who rated out a lot of police officers. For detective Green walking through the homicide unit is like walking through a ghost town. He reach captain Martínez Office. The door was already open. Like usual there is no pictures or Knickknacks hanging up. The office looks so plane. Lieutenant Post is in the office so is the chief of police. Still in his class A uniform. Also captain Martínez. They all stared at him. Detective closed the door.

"The medical examiner said he will work through the night. I am seeing him first thing in the morning." "Good. Did the mother tell you why someone would want her dead?" The captain asked. "No, she was well liked by everyone. the mother didn't know anything." Lieutenant Post cut in. "I am going to say what everyone is thinking." Martínez says. "Maybe she was killed because of her father?" The whole room got silent. Then a huge knock came on the door. A police officer bursts in. It was Ashley. She speaks. "Lieutenant Post. You are needed at the old Remington arms factory. Six bodies were found. After a report of gun shots in the area. Post rose up out of his seat. So did Green.

"We're not done with you detective." The Chief of Police says. Detective Green ignore him and continued. While walking he hears the chief screaming. "Get your ass back here now!" Detective Green continues to ignore him. They reach the car. Lieutenant Post says. "He is going to have your ass for ignoring him." "I don't give a fuck" They both started laughing after detective Green response. They're drove to the Factory. We're there are a sea of people. The police officers are struggling to keep people back. The officers cleared away for Lieutenant Post and Detective Green. Green shows the scene commander his badge and speaks. "I have Lieutenant Post with me." "Attention everyone the lieutenant is on scene." The scene commander says over the radio. They drove up to the factory. It's starting to fall apart. The building looks like all the other abandoned factories in Bridgeport. Run down. They existed the car. While walking to the scene. They are met by one of Post men from his narcotic team. Big muscular guy. Who looks like the Rock. "We meet again detective." "Yes, we do." "Let me get to the point. The men that are dead in them. Are all Gonzalez men."

Green looks at Post. They both have that all shit. Look on their face. "Forensics team is in their now." "Let's keep out and let them do their job. This is our unit case. You know what to do." Post says to his guy. He leaves back to continue to process the scene. You need to find Gonzalez and talk to him. The last thing we want is a war." Detective Green says. "You can leave now. Keep me informed on the progress of your investigation. You shouldn't be near this. Just in case if you're brother is involved." Green nods his head in agreement. Walks back to the car with the mindset of going to Murphy's law. Before he can get into the car. He felt a hand grabbing his shoulder. Then he was spun around violently. He is now face to face with the person who grabbed him. It was the police chief. The chief grabs detective a Green. By the collar lifting him off the ground and pinning him against the car.

"You ever disrespect me like that again. I will fuck you up. You are going to learn to respect me." The chief says with so much hatred in his voice. Lieutenant Post immediately separated them. "Detectives get out of here now." "I will be filling a full complaint." Detective Green says. "Do what you have to do Bitch." After the Chief says that. Green ran towards him. With the intent of doing the chief bodily harm. He is stopped by Lieutenant Post. "He wants you to hit him so he can fire you. Calm down and get out of here." Green finally listens and leaves.

It's a short drive to Murphy's law from the factory. Before Green can get out of the car. A city-wide app went though the radio. Saying. "Mr Gonzalez and Joe Dickerson wanted for questioning in the shooting at the. Remington arm Factory." Green knows that had to be the Chief who gave that order. He gets out of the car and walks to the entrance of Murphy's law. He opens the door immediately the bartender calls out his name. "Michael Green how is it going. The bartender's name is Walter Lombardi older Italian guy who can pass of as Irish. Green walks up to him shakes his hands then says. "Is the owner in? I need to see the security tapes from last night." "Wait right here I will get her." He leaves to get the owner. Detective Green sits at the bar for about three minutes before the owner shows up. Nice, beautiful Irish women. Detective Green had known her for years.

Even when he was living in North Carolina. She gave him and embracing hug. Kisses him on the cheek which gave him a nice smile. "I figure you would be coming down. It's already for you in my office up stairs. Plus hear is a copy of the recording." She hands him a cd. Green has a smile on his face. He walks to her office which is up stairs. He takes the stairs in the back next to the pool tables. He sees a number of people at the pool table. One of the guys look familiar but he can't put his finger on it. The person he thinks he sees is his brother's right hand man Fredric. He walks into the office. There's a lot of pictures of the owner trip to Ireland. He walks to the computer and touch the screen. The video plays he sees Amber holding hands with her boyfriend. Watching the band play.

Then he sees them walk to the bar. Green notices someone watching following them. He sees the boyfriend accidentally bump someone. It looks like a fight is about to happen. Then it is stopped by someone unexpected. Detective Green is shocked by who it is. It is Hector Gonzalez. Son and right-hand man Mr. Gonzalez his father. He sees Hector Walk to the boyfriend and amber. Then escorted them out. Detective Green grabs his cell phone then calls Lieutenant Post. "Hello." "I have something you need to see. Amber may be under the personal protection of Mr Gonzalez. I have it hear on tape." "What in the hell. Where are you." "Murphys Law. I will meet you outside." "I am on my way." Detective Green has a huge smile on his face. He shuts down the computer and walks out of the office. He reaches the bar when he notices someone at the bar waiting for him. "Sit down brother. Let's have a drink together." His brother Joe Dickerson is at the bar.

Detective Green starts to think. He now knows that that was Fredric he saw at the pool table. "Sit down and have a drink brother." Green sat down across from Joe. He was all ready drinking a drink. By the look of the glass. Green suspect it must be rum and coke. The bartender hands Green a drink. "You still drink captain and coke?" Joe asked. Green nods his head yes. Joe has a peculiar smile on his face. Like he is up to something. "You are now a multi millionaire and you still have a job as a police detective. Why won't you just quit? The Chief doesn't want you. Your about to have a baby. By that gorgeous piece of ass cop." Green immediately stands up. He knocks the chair over he was sitting on. Fredric stands in between him and Joe. "Don't even try it Bitch." Fredric says in Green face. Joe taps Fredric on the shoulder. Then says, "calm down before my brother puts you in the hospital."

Fredric moves away. Then Joe walks up to detective Green then says. "Calm down bro I was just complementing you on your taste." They both sat back down. "What do you want? I am a busy person." Green says while taking a sip of his drink. "I just want to see my brother. You never came and thank me for the lawsuit money." Joe said with a smile on his face. "I kind of find it insulting bro." Green slams his drink on the bar. Breaking the glass. Everyone turns and watch what is going on. "I didn't want to take that money, but our father took it for me. He put it in my account. That money is for my unborn child." Detective Green is getting real tense. Joe says to Green very loudly. "Don't you ever call that fucking pale face bastard. Father in my site again. He is no father of mine. You Uncle Tom's mother fucker."

Green grabs Joe by the neck. Squeezing so hard Joe falls to his knees. Out of nowhere two uniformed officers Grabbed Detective Green. Separating them. "Are you okay Mr. Dickerson?" Joe turns around and he sees lieutenant Post. Post continues. "You are wanted Joe for questioning in the shooting at the Old Remington arms factory." Joe begins to laugh. So does Fredric. Both Green and

Lieutenant Post have confused looks on their face. "You can contact officers Smith and Sanchez. They both saw me at Whites Diner having dinner." Joe said with a smile on his face. "Whites diner doesn't open for dinner. Just breakfast and lunch." Detective Green said. "You know brother we both know the owner. Especially after he saved my life when we were kids." Green nods his head yes. Lieutenant Post made a phone call. Then two minutes later he came back. "You are free to go."

Joe and Fredric left with smiles on their face. Before Joe leaves Murphy's he turns around then says to Green. "You put your hands on me like that again. I will forget we are brothers. I still owe you an ass whipping. You remember what you did to me when we were kids." After Joe left lieutenant Post looks at Green then says. "What is he talking about detective?" "Not here let's go." They leave plus the uniforms officers leave also.

CHAPTER 10

Both Green and Post pull up on his house in Trumbull. A town which is next to Bridgeport. A beautiful house with a nice front yard. Football size backyard. Post stands in aww on how gorgeous the house is. "So, you did take the money?" Post said. "My stepfather did and deposit in my banking account. So internal affairs don't be on my ass." Post nods his head in agreement. "Anyway, internal affairs can't do nothing to you anyway. Because that money you got from a lawsuit." "Try telling that to our chief of police." "Good point." Post says with a smile on his face. They both sat on chairs in the front lawn of Green house. Post looks at him and speaks. "Be straight with me detective. I am talking to you as a friend and not as your commanding officer."

Detective Green took a minute. Then he begins to say. "I was in high school. Me and my brother was at central high. I was a sophomore he was a junior." Post stopped him immediately then says with a confused look on his face. "How is that possible? When you are three years older than your brother." "Joe is very smart. Book smart that is. He always got straight A's in school. He was tested and they skipped him a grade. I was the one who always got into fights. I stayed in trouble. Until one day." Post shifts himself in the chair to get comfortable. "There was this one girl Hispanic that was a junior. He was seeing her, but she already had a boyfriend. Her boyfriend just happened to be Mr. Gonzalez son his oldest." Post stopped Green again.

His mouth is covered like someone in shock. "I thought Mr. Gonzalez only had one son. Hector." Green shook his head no. "His oldest son is named Carlos. He is ruthless. A stone-cold killer. Now let me finish my story. Carlos caught Joe kissing his girlfriend. He went off and beat my brother into a coma. Me and my family got to see him in the hospital. I immediately left took the shotgun and left to see Carlos. I was stopped immediately. My father got there in time. They send Carlos to Mexico. They did that because my mother press charges. Still to this day there's a warrant out for his arrest. After my brother got well. My father sent him to boarding school in Long

Island." "Were he met some of the Italians that he has connections with?" Post asks. "Yes. Trust me my brother is smart very smart." Lieutenant Post phone begins to ring he answered it. He spends at least five minutes on the phone. "That was corner. He is expecting you at the medical examiner's Office at ten o'clock in the morning." "I will see you then lieutenant." "We are not done yet. You still didn't tell me what you found on the security camera at Murphy's law." "Sorry I almost forgot." Green smiling while saying that. "Your mind was on that woman you have up stairs. Can't blame you." They both broke out into a laugh. "When I was viewing the tape. I noticed that Hector was following Amber. Actually, more like being a bodyguard." Post looks at detective Green with a confused face. He begins to ponder the same thing Green is pondering. "We need to pick up Hector." Post says. "The question that is on my mind is. If he is her bodyguard? Why would she need one and if he was following her was, he the one that killed her?"

Post picks up his cellphone. Dials a number he talks on it for five minutes. Shoutings out orders giving commands. He then turns to detective Green. "You are coming with me. I have officers picking up Hector now. We will meet them in the interview room." They drove to the Bridgeport police department. Post parked in his personal parking lot. They exited the car and is met by the sergeant on duty. A Hispanic male. Who has been on the force for a decade. "Lieutenant Post, Detective Green we have both suspect's." Both Post and Green look confused. Then green say. "What do you mean both? Your orders was to pick up Hector. No one else." "Who did you pick up?" Post yelled loudly. "We picked up detective Greens nephew David Buckshot." The on duty sergeant says.

"We're the officers who picked him up?" Green says. The sergeant points to two police officers who are heading to their cruiser. The sergeant waving them over. Two Hispanic police officers one is a rookie the other a ten-year veteran. The veteran is a police officer named Luis Andres a very good police officer who could be a detective. But doesn't want to the job. He says it's too political for him. He is well built plus he is a former marine. The rookie is a Hispanic named Alvaro Garcia he was a star high school football player. Plus won many trophies in martial arts particularly Brazilian Jujitsu. He scored off the charts in the exam plus in the academy. They approach Post and Green boldly with no fear.

I am guessing I would get a match." "Put that cup down right now! David don't say anything." "Yea David don't say anything. How long before my brother finds out you pissed on yourself. In front of people who supposed to take orders from you and him." "Michael shut up now this interrogation is over." Michael pushed detective Green into the wall. Lieutenant Post begins to put handcuffs on the lawyer before Green says. "I am not pressing charges let him go." The lawyer Grabs the coffee cup then says. "Don't even try to get DNA from the sweat of his hands on the table. Not without a court order. We will be in touch. Michael Joe's lawyer left with both clients. Once gone Green says to Post. "Get the DNA right now from the table we can't use it, but it will let us know if we are on track." Post agreed.

"I will have a radio car take you home." "I have some typing to do I will sleep in the rooms upstairs." Post agree and detective Green went to his desk and began typing.

CHAPTER 11

Detective Green begins to wake up. He smells sweet perfume the one his girlfriend wears. He can also smell the shampoo she used for her hair. As he opens his eyes, he noticed she is lying next to him. He gets up out of the bed. Which is located in the police department. She is still asleep. He also noticed the clothes she brought. He grabs them and heads to the male locker room to take a shower. On his way there he runs into lieutenant Post. "After you take your shower meet me at the car downstairs. So, we can go to the autopsy." Green nods yes and continues to the shower. Before he walks into the locker room. Someone yelling his name.

He turns to see who is calling him. It's the desk Sargeant. The one on morning shift. Older white male. He has three months left before he retires. "Detective Green your brother left you a message. He said to come to his house in Shelton for dinner." Green taps him on the back while he catches his breath. "I'll be okay detective I am just getting old." Green smiles then says. "You didn't have to run all the way here to tell me that. You could have left a note on my desk." "True detective but your desk is the street." They both started laughing. "True said Sargent true said. We will miss you when you retire. You are the best Sargeant this department ever had." The desk Sargeant smiles from the comment detective Green said. "I have to leave detective. I don't understand this place anymore.

Most of my friends are either in jail or retired. I am surrounded by people I don't know if I can trust. I walk in here everyday with my safety off. Thinking is this going to be the day I kill one of these corrupt cops." Green notices his demeanor changes while he is talking. "You watch your back detective. Don't trust nobody and I mean nobody." Detective Green gives him an embracing hug then they departed ways. Green took his advice to heart. Because he knows that this particular desk Sargeant has a way being invisible. He can be in a room, and no one knows he was even there. Detective Green finished his shower got dressed. Before he leaves the male locker room. He is met by detective Hagan. He has a black eye, there's some blood on his nose. He can tell he has been in a fight. "If I find out you did this to me this time you are going to die." Hagan said loudly. Green grabs him immediately then says. "If you have the balls, do it now." They are immediately separated by Green's brother who is with his lawyer and police chief. "Are you threatening my family detective? I take threats to my family very seriously." Joe said is such a threatening voice it gave chills to everyone. "Hagan go to my office now. You are suspended. As for you detective Green. What do you think you was doing running a DNA test on a suspect without a warrant?" Detective Green had nothing to say. He just stood there in silence. While wondering how his brother finds out so fast.

"I am sorry Mr Dickerson." Joe looks at his brother with a wicked smile on his face. Joe taps his brother on his shoulder while saying. "You don't have to apologize. You were just being overzealous. Besides were brothers. We all we got. You and your girl come by for dinner tonight." Joe turns a walk away. So does the chief. Detective Green heads to the car at the back of the police station. We're he finds lieutenant Post leaning against the car and sipping a cup of coffee. Green continues to walk towards him. While contemplating on how his brother found out about the DNA test. "I know what you are thinking. I heard. Actually, I was there in the chief office. I think we have a leak in the Forensics lab." Post says while taking another sip of coffee. "That means what ever test we run through that lab. Joe will know about."

Detective Green slams his hand on the hood of the car. "I will find the mole on my end. You continue with your investigation. Find out who killed Amber." Green agrees with Post. They both get into the car and head to the medical examiner's office.

JOE DICKERSON:

Joe ordered the driver to take them to the catholic church on Washington Avenue. Frederick already knows why they are going there. "Make sure you take care of our friend in the police department." Joe said while looking out of the window. "I already did. Plus, as usual he is at the gambling spot on Stratford Avenue. Losing it on blackjack." They both begin to laugh. As the the truck came to a stop. Joe exits the Cadillac truck it's a nice sunny day. He walks up to the church. He is met by a white male in a black robe with two crosses on them. One on each side in red. The man is wearing glasses. He has three gold rings on his right hand.

"Welcome my son. This is truly a blessed day." He said with a smile on his face. "First of all, I am not your son. Second don't ever speak to my wife. You want to see me tell Frederick over their." Joe pointing to Frederick who is leaning against the truck. "Joe I am sorry. Very sorry." The priest is very nervous now. He begins to stutter his words. His hands begin to shake. "Calm down calm down." Joe says while patting the priest on the back. "If I wanted you dead who will be." Joe looking him saying this. "Now what do you want?"

"Two of your men came to confession yesterday. They confess in killing Mr Gonzalez and his men. By putting them in a meat grinder." Joe begins to get angry. He knows if they confess to a priest. Then they would confess to the police. Joe waves Frederick over to him. "I want you to write down you confessed. Then give the list to Frederick he knows what to do." Joe turns his head to Frederick. Who nods his head in agreement on what Joe said to the priest. "Also, I am tripling the number of drugs that will be on the plane." The priest looks at him in shock and in disbelief.

"You can't do that. I thought we agreed to bring it in. In small amounts so we can operate under the radar." Joe looks at Frederick then back at the priest. Then says in a loud voice. "You and the church owe me. Your serial killer priest almost killed my brother. His son who on your request I kept hidden at the mental hospital wing at Bridgeport Hospital. Or should I make him known to the world." "Okay okay" The priest cut in knowing the damage it will cause if word gets out that the Catholic Church also has serial killers' dressings as priest. "Now you have a nice day. Oh, and don't worry I know about the arrangement you and Mr Gonzalez has. You will have a fresh batch to the house tomorrow. Frederick will see to it." Joe leaves with Frederick and they both get back in the truck. "Did he give you the list of names?" Fredrick shows him the paper with the names on them. "All five names are all from David crew." You see the expression on Joe's face. He begins to contemplate on what to do. He knows he have to deal with this swiftly.

Plus, in this situation he knows his nephew must die. "Confessions to the Priest is the same as ratings to the cops. The men on that list introduced them the God. My nephew brings him to my office on Stratford Avenue." Fredrick nods in acknowledgement then leaves the truck and begins to walk towards city hall.

Detective Green

Lieutenant Post and Detective Green begin to drive to the corner office. Post hands Green a badge. It reads Sargent on it. "You are going to be head of Robbery Homicide division. After your case and mine there going to be no more narcotics team. Due to budget cuts and they have begun defunding the police department." As Green drives he shakes his head in disgust. "A lot of police officers will leave the force because of this. Some may just retire." Green says. "I know but there is nothing we can do. It's election year and the mayor are doing this to win votes." That's the one thing detective Green hates about this job. Is the politics it ruins the job. "In the academy they tell how you are going to protect and serve. How you are going to help people and enjoy every minute of it.

What they don't tell you is you have to deal with all the political bullshit. You are judged based on what other cops do." "I know detective I know. You have to remember the oath we took." "My training officer told me this one thing. I will never forget what he said. Till this day it's the best advice anyone ever told me. Your failures are known but your success is not. No matter how many lives you saved or criminals you brought down. That won't mean a dam thing in the end." Lieutenant Post reached over to the driver side and pulled the emergency break. Bringing the car to a sudden stop then yells at detective Green. "Don't you ever say that. I don't believe in that shit. Yes, times are tough, and we are being unjustly judged because of crooked police officers." Detective Green put the car back in drive. They continue to the medical examiner's office in silents.

The medical examiners office is located in the basement of Bridgeport hospital. The hospital recently purchases the street in front of it. They converted into a new welcome center. Making it more easer to lockdown the hospital in case of emergency. Detective Green uses valet to have the car parked. Both begin to walk into the hospital. Green noticed a lot of changes. A heavy security in the lobby. Cameras everywhere plus a new welcome desk. They are met by a security officer white well built and supporting a 9 mm. "Can I help you two detectives?" "How you know we are detectives?" Says Lieutenant Post. "I saw detective Green on the news yesterday." Post looks at detective Green who gives Post a I don't know shrug.

"We are going to the medical examiner office." Post announced. "Okay but I have to escort you because you need a special key on the elevator to get there. New security protocol implemented because of the shooting that happened two years ago." Post again looks at detective Green then says. "Remind me to thank Lieutenant Morales in Boston when I get a chance." As soon as they got into the elevator Green says. "How did he become a lieutenant that fast?" "He solved several high-profile cases plus he caught the Boston strangler copycat. He is a dam good detective." Detective Green starts to feel happy for him. After what happened with the hearing. Green knows he is one person that deserve something good.

They continue going down in the elevator. They finally reached the basement. It's well lit and very long. "These tunnels go all over the place. I can go to the clinic and the mental hospital all underground." says the security officer with a smile on his face. They finally reached the door that says medical examiner officer. They can hear jazz music playing inside. The security officer used his badge to unlock the door. They walk into the huge office with nine examinations tables five of the tables are being used. They see Dr Chen finishing up on one of the five. He un gowns his personal protective uniform. Then he washes his hands. He walks to them. "Hello detective Green and hello lieutenant Post. You guys have been keeping me busy these past 24 hours. The slugs I pulled from the Remington Arms shooting I sent to forensic last night. Those slugs match the ones from a cold case homicide last year." Chen hands lieutenant Post a thick file. Detective Green gives Post a perplex look. Lieutenant Post glances at the file. "I remember this case. Double homicide last year. In the Pt Barnum houses." "Then my brother is the prime suspect." "I agree but finding evidence on him is going to be tough." Green nods his head in agreement.

"Follow me detective." They follow Dr Chen to Amber willcots body. Chen removes the sheet that was covering the body. "Dam she has some nice tits." Chen and Post gives Green a cold glance. "Show some respect Detective." Chen says. "She is completely healthy. Except for this needle mark on he left in the neck right in the jugular vain." They both look and see what the Dr is talking about. They both notice the small needle mark on her neck. "This woman was poisoned. The killer uses a syringe most likely an epipen. A lot of assassins in China, Japan, and Hong Kong use this method."

Both Green and lieutenant Post look at each other. "This was a hit. Do you know what kind of poison killed her?" Green asked. "No the poison was fast acting very fast. If there is another body. You must get me the body in under ten minutes." Chen says. The phone rings and Chen walks away to answer the phone. "My brother didn't do this. He is cold hearted but he didn't do this." "I agree Mr Willcots is at north end correctional. You go and tell him what we know so far." Post says. Chen returns with a sorry look on his face. Both Green and Post can see the frustration on his face. They're been a lot of murders this year in Bridgeport plus his staff was cut in half because of budget cuts.

"Three people was found dead in Newfield Park. All three with there throat slashed from ear to ear with a rat in their mouth. I told the scene commander I will tell you lieutenant Post." "I am coming with" Detective Green says.

Chapter 12

They pulled up on the crime scene at Newfield Park on Newfield Avenue. Usually there is kids playing basketball at on of the six hoops. Or people playing horseshoe at the other end. Nobody uses the tennis court anymore. Detective Green decided to park the car in the police academy parking lot. Both Green, lieutenant Post and Dr. Chen exit the car. They are met by the captain of the police academy. Captain Richards a 25-year veteran of the force. Was sent to work here after twenty-six bricks of cocaine turns up missing in the evidence locker.

Captain Vincent couldn't connect him to the disappearance of the drugs. Sent him here then a week later the captain Vincent is found dead. Captain Richard reached us finally. He is out of breath and overweight. "There's a LA Fitness about a five-minute drive from here." They all laughed at what detective Green said. "I have the cadets helping to keep people from the crime scene. The mailman discovered the bodies. He called me directly and we locked the area down immediately. I have officers going door to door asking questions. Also, detective Hagan is being put in charge of the investigation."

Both Green and Post has that what the fuck look on their face. "The word came down from the chief lieutenant." Richard says. "Thanks captain. Green gets out of here. If Hagan sees you there is going to be problems." Post says in concern. "Once I identify the victims I will leave. They began to walk to Newfield Park. They cut through the police academy and the church next door. To avoid people and the news media. The duck under the crime scene tape they could see the bodies. Dr. Chen is already there doing his thing. They could see detective Hagan talking to the mailman.

As they approach the bodies. Detective Green gets a chill up his spine. He recognized all three victims. Detective Hagan joins them then says. "Three male victims dead with their throats slashed from ear to ear. With a rat in their mouths. They have no identification on them." "Michael Brown, Jackson Marley, and Jim Buddins." Green cut in. "How did you know that Sargent and congrats on your promotion." Hagan says. "I almost had them on a rape charge, but the victim recanted. Tell the crime scene guys to make sure they take their DNA plus fingerprints. We might be able to close some cold cases." Lieutenant Post nods his head in agreement. Green leaves them and heads back to the car so he can go to the correction facility on North Avenue in Bridgeport

Detective Green doesn't like Hagan still. He costs him a job with the F.B.I and tired to get him fired. Then he reveals secrets he learned from his time at cold case unit and 911 operations. To keep his job which further hurt the police department. Which helped people push for defunding the police department. As he approached his police issued vehicle. He sees captain Richard talking to someone in a blacked-out SUV. Green pulls his phone out and begins to record. He gets the license plate and the vehicle and captain Richard. He sees a hand reach out handing Richard a large envelope. Been gets that on video also.

The vehicle leaves and gets waved through the police checkpoint. Captain Richard opens the envelope and Green can see a lot of cash in captain Richards hands. He has a huge smile on his face. He then proceeds to enter the police academy. Detective Green puts his phone away and continue to his police issued vehicle. He then makes a mental note to talk to lieutenant Post and show him the video he took. Green begins to think that Captain Richard probably helps put those bodies in Newfield Park. He climbs into his vehicle and heads to the prison.

CHAPTER 13

Detective Green arrived at North end Correctional. Upon arrival he notices. A black SUV the same one he saw captain Richards talking to. He exits the car and begins to walk slowly to the prison entrance. He walks pass the black SUV. As soon has he can get a look at the driver's side widow. The tinted windows went up to block his view. Green walks more quickly to the entrance. He sees prisoners mopping floors and emptying trash cans. He walks up to one of the receptions at the desk. He identifies himself and shows his badge.

A person in a nice gray suit came to meet him. He looks a little young but fit. Especially for a white male. "Hello, I am Warden Jonathan Rams. Mr Willcots is in one of our interrogation rooms. His lawyer is in their with him. They have been complaining on when y'all will release the body. The district attorney is on the way." Green nods his head and begins to follow the Warden. They arrived at the interrogation room. Green and the Warden didn't speak on the walk to the interrogation room. He walks in the room. He sees Mr. Willcots former district attorney for the city of Bridgeport.

He also sees his brother's attorney Michael. "Hello detective Green." Says Michael with a smile. Green sits down then says. "I know you want the release of the body of your daughter. He body is all yours. The chief medical examiner has been busy. That's why you weren't able to get in touch with him." "Thanks, I will call the funeral home after this." Michael said. "Next time you fucking Italian fuck. You call me directly you would have been had the body." Green says "I told you to call him. I know detective Green he is honorable." Says Mr Willcots while looking at his lawyer. His lawyer turns and looks at Willcots then says. "If you new him before he became a police officer. You would think differently."

Mr. Willcots looks at detective Green with much fear. Then he says. "I heard rumors of your past detective. The story I have heard gives me nightmares. That your more of a killer than the Iceman who was a for the mob." "We are here about your dead daughter not me Mr. Willcots. By the way according to the medical examiner your daughter was poisoned. Who would want to kill your daughter?" After detective Green said that Willcots stood up and started crying.

He begins to pound his fist against the wall. His lawyer grabs him to calm him down. It took ten minutes, but he finally calms down. "Who would want to hurt my daughter? She was a good girl. Straight A student full scholarship." Willcots says with tears in his eyes. "Maybe you are the target. They couldn't get to you in prison, so they went after your daughter." Willcots stood up with his hands over his mouth. He looks at his lawyer then says. "Who ever wants to kill me they can get to me in prison easy. Plus, they promised to leave my family alone." "Who are they Mr. Willcots?" Green says in excitement. "This interrogation is over. Guard on the gate." Michael yells out. Then the guard grabs Willcots and escorted him back to his cell.

Detective Green exit the the correctional facility he walks into the district attorney. He is wearing a blue suit, and he has a decent size file in his hands. He took over the job after mr Willcots got arrested. He is actually better than Willcots. With an amazing 92% conviction rating and is in line for a judge position. Green approach the district attorney then said. "The interrogation is over. His attorney won't let him speak anymore." Green sees the frustration on his face. He explained what happened then the district attorney says. "I will try. Hopefully he will tell me who he is covering for. Since he believes they killed his daughter even though it is not true." He leaves for the correctional facility leaving detective Green by himself.

Green gets into the the car. He figures he will go and talk to one of Ambers friends to get more information. One of them is his brother's stepdaughter. He will go see her at her house on East Main Street. At this time of the day, she should be at the Catholic Church she volunteers there. She has been doing that for the past ten years. He starts the car and begins to head for the church. While driving dispatch calls him over the radio. "This is detective Green go ahead." "Lieutenant Post wants you to meet him in front of police department." "Okay heading there now." Green drives for the police department where he finds lieutenant Post in front. Post climbs into the car then says.

"Heads up Hagan is filling a complaint against you." Green stops the car abruptly while several cars pass them honking their horns. "What the hell did I do? All I did was help him with his investigation." Green says. "He doesn't see it that way. He thinks you are trying to take over his investigation. Plus, he still believes you are helping your brother by feeding him information." Green punches the steering wheel very hard. Lieutenant Post trying his best to calm him down. Then out of nowhere a knock came on the window of the car. It's a uniformed officer. They rolled down the window then lieutenant Post showed his badge. The officer backed off and left them. Green continued to drive to the Catholic Church on east Main Street. They arrived at the Catholic Church where they see Cinthia Ramos sitting on the church's steps talking to one of the nuns. He can see tears in her eyes. Green guess that it is probably because of Amber. They were close friends in high school. Always hanging out doing everything together. Along with their other two friends.

Ramos has been volunteering at the Catholic Church for about six years now. She planted all the plants and the apple tree. Which everyone in the neighborhood comes to pluck apples from. She has been in the newspaper and on Tv for the things she has done here at the Church. My brother is very proud of her so am I. She goes to Fairfield University We're she is on the dean's list and is going to school to be a nurse. Green waited till she finished talking to the nun. Then Green gets out of the along with lieutenant Post. He approaches her cautiously then says. "Hello, did I come at a bad time?" She looks up and sees detective Green. She smiles and grabs him to hug him so tightly Green ribs were hurting.

"I love you to and I miss you. I am sorry to bother you but." "You want to talk about Amber." She cut in and spoke. "Yea do you know anyone who would want to hurt her?" "No, I don't. Actually, I don't before her death we weren't hanging out like that anymore." Green looks at lieutenant Post then back at her. "But y'all was so close?" "I think it's because she didn't get a scholarship to Fairfield University Like I did. Then there was that thing with her father. He gets locked up on corruption charges. Her last year at high school was horrible. The whispers behind her back. No one Wanted to hang out with her but me. But ever time I did daddy gets mad at me."

"He was trying to protect you. He was being a father." "I know uncle G but she was my best friend. She had no enemies but there was that thing our sophomore yea in school." "What thing?" Lieutenant Post says. "You are not supposed to talk to her without her lawyer present." Green recognizes the voice. He turns around to see his brother. He has one of the Catholic Priest with him. They both stand right in front of each other looking each other in the eye. Like they are getting ready to fight. Then out of nowhere a nun comes between them separates them then says. "Not here now. This is the lord's holy place. Mr Dickerson go with the father in the church. Detective Green, I will escort you and lieutenant Post back to your shitty car." They all look at the nun after she made that comment about the car. Then she says. "It is look at it it's a piece of crap. My sister has a better car, and she is a New Haven police officer." "I didn't know you have a sister?" The Catholic priest says. She continues to escort them back to the car then she whispers in Detective Green ear. "YMCA incident six years ago" Then she hurries back to the other side of the church. Lieutenant Post and detective Green gets in the car.

Green then tells lieutenant Post what the nun said. He was just as puzzled as the detective is. "I can't recall anything that happened there six years ago." Lieutenant Post says. "I will look into it. If my brother is here. He is planning the funeral." "Yes, he is, and I don't want you there. You and the Catholic Church don't get along." Green smiled and started the car. While in the car the phone for lieutenant Post was ringing. He answered it he had a smile on his face in the beginning of the car. Then a frown towards the end of the call. He hangs up the phone. Then he says. "Excellent job on asking for a DNA search on the victim's this morning.

All three victims DNA came back on several open cases. Mainly Murder cases. Especially those trans murders." After lieutenant Post finished what he was saying. Green slams his hand on the steering wheel. Detective Green worked those cases. Now he has to go back to update the file. Plus have a conversation with detective Hagan. A conversation he didn't want to have.

CHAPTER 14

Joe Dickerson watched as his brother pulls off. He turns to his daughter who is sitting on the bench. He sits next to her kissing her on her fore head. She wipes it off like a person does when they are too old for something. "What questions did your uncle ask you?" Joe asking her in a tone that made her feel safe. "He ask me who would want to hurt Amber and why." Joe turned and looked at Fredric then at the sky like a person in deep thought. "Go home and get ready for the funeral tomorrow." She got up and walk to her car. Joe single for two people that was with him to watch her.

Joe got up and walked to Fredric. Then he paused for a little then says. "I want you to hold the fort down I need to go see a prisoner. You know which one I am talking about." Fredric nods his head in approval. Joe walks to his car then begins to make a phone call. Before he finished dialing the number Fredric knocks on the window. Joe rolls the window Down. "Maybe we should wait? We don't know yet if he has anything to do with this. Plus, there is only one victim, and your brother still thinks she may have enemies." Fredric says while catching his breath.

Joe pause for a long time contemplating what Fredric just said. He agrees with what he says. Then Joe says. "If there are any more victims then I will pay him a visit." "For the record Joe you should have killed him a long time ago. Native Americans always say When You Have a chance to kill your enemy You do it. You let your father rot in prison. For what I don't know but it can come back and bite us in the ass one day." Fredric warns Joe who begins to smile. He reaches out of the window pats him on the shoulder then says. "Don't worry I have everything under control. Now get in the car we have a Funeral to plan for tomorrow." He gets in the car and they drove off.

CHAPTER 15

Detective green sat at his desk updating his case files. He now has no open cases. Since the three that bodies at Newfield park were his prime suspect. He found out when the DNA came back. Green told himself he would notify the victims of his open cases. On what is going with their respective cases. He just finished updating the last file when a knock came at his office door. He looked up and he see's lieutenant Post. His eyes are red he looks a little disheveled and worn out. Green can tale he is tired and exhausted. He looks up at the clock and it reads 9:00pm.

Detective Green didn't realize how late it is. He offered him a seat. Instead, lieutenant Post plopped on the couch in Green's office. "Do you need a blanket lieutenant?" "No, I need you to come with me to captain Martinez office. He wants to talk to you plus bring those files on your desk. Those will make excellent readings material for detective Hagan." Green started smiling after he heard what Post said. Green has been typing since he came back from the Catholic Church on East Main Street. For nine hours he has been typing. The only good thing is he now has an office since he is going to be the supervisor in charge for the Homicide unit.

"How did Hagan respond when he found out I am his new boss?" "He immediately ran to the chief and ask for a transfer. Which was denied. The chief did let him investigate the previous murders that was similar." "I should be investigating those murders." "You can't detective because it may lead back to your brother. Come on let's go to the captain's office I will take half of those file while you grab the other half." They grabbed the files and begin walking to Martinez office.

It is a skeleton crew on the homicide unit. The night watch of detective at their desk. Some are typing others are making follow up calls for the day watch. The watch commander is at his desk drinking coffee. He yells out to detective Green. "When you get a chance detective come and see me." Green nods in approval as he continues to Martinez office. His door is already open. He has the look of a person that is getting ready to go home. His office is still bear with no pictures or nothing on the wall. It still looks like he just moved into the office. He see's the files Green and Post are carrying. Martinez gave them both an annoying look. He takes his coat off and put it back on the coat rack. Lieutenant Post says immediately before Martinez can say anything. "These are a result of the DNA match that came back on the victim's. From that Newfield park thing." Martinez start to smile then he says. "I will happily give all these case files to detective Hagan. Also detective Green don't bother doing the follow ups on these cases. Hagan can do it all of it. Victim notification the family everything.

How does it feel to have only one open case? Which is the one your working on." Green is starting to see were this is going. "I am doing fine I have no suspects yet." The tension in the room starting to get thick. "If you can't handle this case I can give it to someone else?" "No you tell my brother and the Catholic Church. They are not getting rid of me that easily." Detective Green stands up and begin to leave. When captain Martinez says. "I haven't dismissed you sergeant get your ass back in that chair." Green looks at Martinez then he begins to charge him. He is stopped by lieutenant Post. Then Post says. "What is going on captain?"

"I heard about your little trip to East Main Street stay away from the Catholic Church. That is a direct order." Post escort Green out of the Martinez office. They continued till they reach the watch commander. The watch commander rose from his seat. He approached lieutenant Post and Green. "I heard the yelling from here. Please tell me you punched that political hack?" The watch commander says while giving Green a cup of water. "No, I didn't I should have but didn't." Says Green with a smile on his face. "He is trying to be chief of police. That is why he has been a total ass. No body in the department likes him.

He has been playing politics for a while now. I will let detective Hagan know about the files you gave to captain Martinez. Most like he will comb through them to find something to blame you. So he can score political points." Detective Green pats him on the back as a thank you. Him and lieutenant Post continued to detective Green's office. We're they are met by one of lieutenant Post men. In his unit a unit that is about to be disbanded. Detective Green knows him as the Rock because of his body. He is shaped like the iconic movie star.

He is sitting at Green's desk with a file in his hands. "I heard the yelling, so I decided to come to your office. Those bodies at Newfield Park. Their DNA matched blood found at our crime scene. At the old Remington factory. Which means they was their." "Did you find any fingerprints on the scene?" Detective Green asked. "Yea about a dozen a lot of homeless people." "What about from the shell casings found on the scene?" "I never bothered to check. We have the shell casings in the evidence. I will have them checked." "Make sure you use the FBI labs not ours." Lieutenant Post says "By the way detective please call me detective Hannan. Not the Rock even though I do look like him." They all laugh while detective Hannan leaves.

He closes the door when he leaves. Leaving lieutenant Post and detective Green alone. Green reached in his pocket, and he finds a note. He pulls it out and shows it to lieutenant Post. They both wonder who it is from, but they know who put the note in Green's pocket. It was the watch commander. "It looks like he still got it. All those years in robbery paid off." Post says with a smile on his face. Green reads the note which says. Meet me at Whites Diner at 9:00am we need to talk. Green looks at Post gives him a shrug. "You meet this person tomorrow and stay at the diner till the funeral is done since it's right down the street." Post says. Green agrees with him. Then he grabs his coat to leave for the day.

CHAPTER 16

Lauren Scrolls views the picture of her friend Amber. She starts to remember all the good times they had in high school. The dances, party's, skipping school to hangout all day at the mall. Ever since she started college, they all drifted apart. The only friend she still sees on the regular is Tasha Young. They both go to Fairfield University. Actually, they are roommates in the same dorm. Tasha going to school for a business degree. Lauren still remembers getting the notification on Amber death while she was doing her clinical at Yale New Haven hospital. The floor she is doing her clinical said they will higher her once she completed her nursing program.

Tears Start coming down her eyes. Lauren begins to cry because she still feels sorry for not apologize to Amber. On their senior year of high school. Amber's father a prominent lawyer in the district attorney office. Was arrested on corruption charges, taking bribes. She and her other three friends Cinthia, Jessica, and Tasha pretend not to know her. So, we can remain popular in the school. "I am sorry I waited too late. To make amends with you Amber. I am really sorry." Lauren said to the picture of Amber while crying her eyes out. She continues to cry until she hears the phone ring. She dries her eyes and answers the phone.

She recognized the voice as her father Jeremiah Scrolls. The district court judge. Her father's been a judge for a long time. He could have been on the state supreme court. He turned it down. He never gave a reason why despite everyone in the state wanted him to have the job. "We're, are you? Everyone is here at the church the funeral has begun." Lauren's father said sounding worried. "I am leaving now I had a busy night at the hospital." "Okay get here fast okay I love you." Lauren hangs up the phone and hurries to her car. She noticed the back door unlocked. She stairs at it for a moment then shrugged it of. Hopped in her BMW and headed for the Catholic Church on Washington Avenue.

She drives down Main Street heading to the church. Traffic is light for a Thursday morning. She plays some jazz music to come herself down. She starts to get nervous as she nears the church. Tears again begins to fall down her eyes. She finally reached the church but there is no parking. She decided to park in front of Kobe high school. She parks her car then she starts to breathe in and out so she can calm down. The she feels a sting in her neck. "May gods have mercy on your soul." The killer exists the car through the back seat of the car. The killer continues down the street to vine street. Then gets into a waiting car then drives off.

CHAPTER 17

Detective Green pulls into Whites Diner parking lot. There's a lot of cars parked in the lot. Plus, Green recognizes a police cruiser. He exits the car and walks to the diner's entrance. "Welcome back detective. I haven't seen you in a while." Green recognizes the waitress from the last time he was here. He greets her with a smile. "There is a lady waiting for you. She has been here for about ten minutes. Follow me." He begins to follow her to the table. She leads him to the far end of the diner her back is facing them, but he recognizes her by her uniform. She is a nun most likely from the church on east main st.

Soon as he sat down his whole mood change. It's the nun that looks after his niece when she comes to the church to volunteer. "What's wrong? Is she ok?" She taps him on the hand then she says. "For now, yes. Ever since her friend was killed old feeling started to come up. Some of the things she says doesn't make sense. After you left from talking to her. She asked me to take her confession. I told her I can't but one of the priests can. Then she yells not please they can't take my confession. They are not right. Then I said what do you mean? Then she said you know. You just choose to ignore it.

I new what she was talking about. I took her confession and there is something you need to know. Your brother helped cover up a murder that her and her friends did six years ago." Detective Green was shocked and taken back by what the nun said. Then out of know where a hand slams on the table which made both Green and the nun jump. "I thought that was you detective. What are you doing talking to a nun?" It was two police officers. Detective Green recognize both police officers. Officer Andres and officer Garcia. Green figures they must of finished their breakfast. "It's non of your concern." The officers leave with a questionable look on there face. With out realizing it the nun was gone. She disappeared very quickly. Green followed the officers. He continues to stare at them with a hard look.

Green felt a tap on his shoulder. He sees it's lieutenant Post who tells him. "Don't do it. Trust me don't do it. I know that look on your face. Tell me what happened in the diner. Come to think about it I haven't had breakfast let's go in and eat." They both go into the diner and sit at the same table Green and the nun sat in. Detective Green told lieutenant Post what happened from the conversation with the nun up to the interruption by the the police officer. "Do you think it's connected with your case?" Post ask. "I don't know but if we get another victim and it's one of the girls I will look into it very heavy." Lieutenant Post nodded his head in agreement.

Lieutenant Post continues to eat his breakfast that the waitress brought him. Scrambled eggs and bacon with coffee. The waitress brings another cup of coffee for Lieutenant Post and detective Green. When a hand grabs Post coffee and then yells. "Bring two more sweetheart." Lieutenant Post nods his head in agreement. The other gentlemen in detective Hannan. "I have been up all night with the forensic team at the FBI. The finger prints on the shell casings came back to a man named Trell Fredric." Lieutenant Post and detective Green have a shocked look on their face. Post begins to smile like a kid you got what they want for Christmas.

"Go pick him up but first get a arrest warrant for murder multiple counts." Lieutenant Post said still sporting the smile. "No need for a warrant he is on parole. He has a year left we can violate him." Hannan said. "Still get the warrant anyway. He is the right hand man for Joe Dickerson and I don't want to give his lawyer any room to try to get him off." Post says. Detective Hannan leaves in a run and is out the door. Detective Green paid the tab. Him and lieutenant Post head for the door. We're they are met by the same two police officers that startled detective Green. "You both are needed at Kobe High school. A body is found inside a car. The body is identified as the Judges daughter." Post looks at Green. Before he can say anything Green says. "We need to put officer on the other girls. So they will not be the next victim"

Post agree with him and gave direct orders to the police officer to do what detective Green said. They left with lights blazing. "I will meet you at the crime scene." Post says in a soft voice like he was going to cry.

CHAPTER 18

Detective Green pulls into Kobe High School from the Vine Street side which is Calhoun Pl. A small narrow St with a couple of houses on it only in the beginning of the street. Green parks his car at the beginning of the Block. Due to that the street is narrow and it is a must to secure the crime scene. As he exits the car he is met by a gorgeous Hispanic woman in a blue suit. She has long black hair. She is wearing he badge around her neck. She has beautiful hazel eyes with an athletic body. Green felt a tap on his shoulder then a voice says. "She is fine as hell. Has a gorgeous body but remember your girlfriend has a gun detective." Both started laughing then Green turns to his right and sees it is lieutenant Post.

She shook their hands then says. "Hello I am Detective Sanchez Candela Sanchez." Green looks at her with a Familiar look like someone who recognizes someone but don't remember where. "I was assigned as your partner by captain Martinez." "I can't be your partner. I am head of Robbery Homicide." "You have been reassigned. Lieutenant Post doesn't have the authority to put you in that position. Plus you are unqualified." Captain Martinez said very boldly Green starts to rush captain Martinez but is stoped by Post and Sanchez. Post whispers in his ear and is saying. "Don't give him the satisfaction. I will talk to the chief." Green calms down and walks to the crime scene with Post and Sanchez.

Detective Green gives captain Martinez a hard stare as he pass him. As they walk to the crime scene they are met by a young officer who looks new. At least to Green and Sanchez. "Hello detectives and lieutenant. This one is a VIP." Green stops him before he can say anything else then says. Right to his face like a drill Sargent yelling at a soldier. "Every victim is a VIP." "Continue officer." Post says. "We have a white female found dead in her car. Unknown how she died. She was rushed to the morgue by Dr Chen. He said you would know why." Both Green and Post nods their head. "The female name is Lauren Scrolls." After the officer said the name Green put his hands on his head. He begin to cry while Post and Sanchez grab him so he will not fall.

"I am not crying because of Ms Scrolls. I am crying because my niece may be the next victim." Green says. "Officer he are a list of names put a uniformed detail on them ASAP." The officer leaves yelling out commands over the radio. They walk closer to the car to take a look inside. Several crime scene techs are dusting for fingerprints and looking for DNA. Or anything that can help find the killer. The same police officer came back to them then said. "The person you found the body was her father the Honorable Judge Scrolls. He is over near your brother detective Green" Green and Post looks in the direction the officer was pointing. They both see the Judge crying very deeply in Joe Dickerson arms.

They both walk in their direction with detective Green leading the way. Once they approach. The judge continues to cry and standing next to him is Joe Dickerson, with Fredric and Dickersons lawyer. "Right now, the judge is in no fame of mind to talk right Michael." The Lawyer said to detective Green calling him by his first name. "We have to do this. Weather he is ready or not. We are trying to catch a killer." Lieutenant Post says in a commanding tone. Joe sensing the tension in the air. Moves his way to the front then says. "This man just found his own daughter dead in the car. Plus, we just came from a funeral around the corner. We're a close friend of the family and Ambers body still in the church." Joe says very passionately.

A man in a gray jacket that says CSI. A white male that has that biker look on him. Sporting some tattoos. "We have a problem lieutenant Post. There's seems to be no damage to the locks on the car. No finger prints except for the victim. But the backseat on the floor is covered in sweat." "We call 911 last night. We thought we heard someone in the house." The judge says while still wiping tears down his eyes. "How long was the car in the garage?" Detective Green asked "The car never left the garage. She stayed on campus and road to her clinical with your niece detective." After hearing that Green looks towards his brother. Before he can say anything. "She is already under protection. So if you sent a police detail call them off." Joe said with a lot of emotion in his voice.

"That is not going to happen. Plus, we need to question her security detail. They might have seen the suspect and didn't know it." Lieutenant Post responded. "I will make arrangements lieutenant. I also figure you want to question mr Dickerson daughter again." Post nods his head yes. As soon as that happens several police officers came and arrest Fredric. The judge, Joe and the lawyer begins to scream out. As Fredric is lead away in handcuffs. Detective Green and lieutenant Post walks back to the crime scene. While Joe is screaming at them. "I am going back to the police department to handle interrogation of Fredric." Lieutenant Post says as he walks away. Then a police officer approach detective Green. A regular uniform officer. "During our canvas of the scene we noticed this." He points to one of the windows in the school and noticed a camera in the window. "Get the principal or who ever is in charge we need to look at that camera.

Detective Green and detective Sanchez waited for about an hour until a man escorted by a police officer came. He was an elderly white male wearing a mechanic uniform that was stained with a black substance. Green figure it is motor oil. "Thanks for coming in." Green says with a smile. "You took me away from my son's race car I am fixing. He is racing tonight in Stafford." The guy says with an angry tone. He opens the school the door and they begin to follow him. Green walks in the school looking around at the plain walls few trophies in the trophy case. He feels a tap on his shoulder he turns and look. "Is everything okay?" Sanchez asked with such concern. "Yea I am fine. When I was little my mother wanted me to go to this school. My father fight with her and I ended up in Central high school."

They ended up at the classroom. The guy unlock the door the detective walks past him hoping that the camera is still recording. They approach the camera and found it's still recording. They ordered the crime scene tech to take the camera. The guy said he will notify the teacher. Green and Sanchez leave the school and head to the Judge's house. They arrive at the Judges house crime scene techs are already their. Green and Sanchez exit the car. One of the techs came towards them. A nerdy white man with glasses. "The killer got in Through the garage window. The killer must of timed in perfectly when the Judge came home and entered the passcode for the home alarm system."

Both Green and Sanchez looked at each other with puzzled looks. Then detective Green says. "The killer must have watched them to know what time they leave and come home. Question when they came home and dialed 911 because they heard a noise. When our officers came to investigate. Would they have caught the suspect?" "Definitely yes detective. If they would have followed proper procedure and check the garage, they would have found the suspect" Both Green and Sanchez look at each other then Sanchez says. "Who were the idiots that didn't do their job?" "They are over their with their union delegate. Officer Andres and Officer Garcia." Green has a smile on his face. Sanchez looks at him with a beleaguered look. "Make sure you file a full report. Then hand it over to the chief. Those two fucks just screwed the whole department." Green and Sanchez head back in the car and head back to the police station.

Chapter 19

Detective Green and Sanchez are in the car heading back to the police department. While Green is driving, he sees Sanchez reading a police file. He takes a quick glimpse and sees it's the current case. Mainly Amber Willcots. Green can tell she is deep in thought. Green is not worried because maybe she sees something he didn't. He knows he need to talk to the other girls mainly his brother's daughter. Especially after the conversation he had with the nun. "We need to talk to your brother's daughter. I think she is hiding something. We need to talk to her before we talk to the other girls." Green has a smile on his face. Because he was just thinking the same thing. Except she doesn't know about the conversation with the nun.

Sanchez sees the smile on his face. "Let me guess? You was just thinking that wasn't you?" Laughing while she says it. Green nods his head yes. "My last partner kept getting mad I was doing that. I don't know how I do it. I just do it I have been doing it since I was little." Green chuckles then says. "You must know how to read people. You do it without knowing you do it." They pull into the police department parking lot. They use the back entrance we're they are met by the chief of police. Green can tell he is not happy because of the look he has on his face. Plus he is wearing his New York Yankee jersey. Which means he will miss the Yankee game and those tickets are very expensive.

"Is it true?" "Yes, everything Sanchez is about to file a report." Green explained to the chief. He then looks at Sanchez then says. "Go file your report put everything in it then hand it to me and report to Internal Affairs. Don't worry you are not in trouble. I asked them to investigate those officers." "Do you think that is a bit much chief? Suspended them don't and give them a reprimand. All internal Affairs will do is find a way to fire them and charge them." The police chief got red in the face then slam his hand on the door. Breaking the window. "I am the chief I make the orders around here." Saying it so loud everyone within ear shot heard it. Green takes his gun out of the holster and passes it to Sanchez. "You get loud like that with me again. I will beat you like the Bitch you are."

Green says that right in his face. The chief grabs Green by the Collar Then says. "You little shit." Before he can do anything Green rams his head into the chief's nose breaking it. Pools of blood rushes from his face. Numerous police officers rush in. They escort the chief and called an ambulance. "What the fuck just happened?" Green look up and sees it's Lieutenant Post "it's not his fault lieutenant I saw everything." Sanchez says in Green defense. "I have everything on camera Lieutenant detective Green is in the right." Says the watch commander. "Go and type both reports Sanchez. This incident and the other one. Internal Affairs are already on the way."

Sanchez leave then Post says to detective Green. "Let's talk while we go to interrogation room one." When they walk pass interrogation room one Green notice his nephew in the room along with his brothers lawyer. He sees Fredric in room two by himself. "I have internal Affairs picking up the head of the Police academy. Now lets see if we can break Fredric." Before they can walk in the the interrogation room. They are met by captain Martinez. "Don't worry about the incident with the chief I saw the video." Green continue into the interrogation room without saying anything.

Fredric has his hands clenched together while his left leg was moving slightly fast. Post and Green sit down then Green begins to say. "We got you now. My brother's lawyer can't save you this time." "You know those bodies we found at the Remington factory that's near Seaside Park. The bullet Casings have you fingerprints on them." Says lieutenant Post after Green spoke. Fredric continues to sit and not make a move. Except for that left leg which is moving a little faster. "You are going to jail. You violated your parole. Now we are going to add murder charges." Green says. "I didn't commit no murder. I was never there. I was at a barbershop." "You don't have to be their idiot. Your fingerprint on the shell casings makes you and accessory." Post said loudly. "That's not all plus. Those men killed were Gonzalez men. Speaking of Gonzales he is missing." Green said. "Did you and Joe kill him?"

Fredric eyes looked down and his left leg stopped moving. Detective Green begins to sense fear on him. Fredric has the look now of a little kid who is frightened. Green and Post both look at each other then Green says. "That's not all. The bodies we found at Newfield Park. They were the shooters. Looks like the geniuses never threw away the guns they used. We have a witness that place you at the scene dumping the bodies. You are done. That witness is a cop that is going to jail." Detective Green shows him the video of Fredric paying off the the captain. Fredric start pacing back and forth acting very nervous. "Okay I will talk but you have to put me in witness protection program." Then out of nowhere Michael Vintoro comes in and begins yelling. "How dare you question my client without his attorney. Leave now so I can talk to my client. Shame on you Michael." Green and Post leaves the interrogation room but before Green leaves, he says. "Don't you ever call me by my government name." Soon as they leave the room captain Martinez says. "You can blame mr Jack ass over here." Martinez pointing at detective Hagan. "He notified the attorney that you were talking to his client." Both Post, Green and Martinez look at Hagan with such hatred and anger. Post grabs Green shoulder preventing him from charging at Hagan.

Hagan feeling the tension in the room leaves immediately. "Don't worry detective Green. After this I am sending him to the cold case unit. Which is in the basement." They all laughed at what captain Martinez said. Then the district attorney arrived with a face that was cold as ice. Green figures he must of heard of the screw up of detective Hagan. "I have heard detective. At least this time it wasn't you. Plus I got Mr. Willcots talking. He said if you can catch the person who killed his daughter. He will testify against your brother Joe Dickerson." After hearing what the district attorney said everyone in the room was shocked. Then both Post and Captain Martinez say. "Go find out who is doing these killings. You need anything you have it. Plus Sanchez stays as your partner."

Green begins to walk away when he ran into detective Sanchez. "I typed up everything and put it on the captain's desk. I saw that they arrested the captain of the police academy?" Detective Green nods his head yes. Sanchez continues by saying. "Plus I heard their arresting Fredric for multiple counts of conspiracy to commit murder. With one of them being Mr Gonzalez." Green starts to look at her skeptically. Because of the questions she is asking. Both Green and Sanchez see Buckshot leave with his lawyer. Green notices the look on Buckshot face. Like someone who sees a ghost. Before Green can ask what's wrong he is stopped by his lawyer.

"Is everything okay?" Green turns to see it is Sanchez who ask him the question. "I need you to go through every police file to see if we have a record or anything on our two victims and their friends. I will be doing the same thing." She agrees with him then says. "First I need to get something to eat." Sanchez leaves detective Green to head for her car. She enters her car which is parked across the street at city hall what is left of city hall. City hall is moving to a new building. This building is practically empty except for a few things. She sees it's noon time she would probably get lunch at the new Brazilian restaurant downtown. Ass soon she gets into the car and closed the door. A gun cocks back and she feels something metal on the back of her head.

Fear starts to grip her body and she starts praying to god to save her life but she says it in Spanish. "You can stop praying to god he can't save you. Depends on what happens in the next 60 seconds. you can meet him personally." Sanchez recognize the voice.

Chapter 20

Detective Sanchez recognize the voice in the back seat as Joe Dickerson. Who the other person was that has a gun to the back of her head she doesn't know. Nervous and afraid she tries to remain tough. "Let me guess it was Ms Gonzalez that had you spy on my brother?" Sanchez nods her head yes. While taking a quick glance at her picture of her two girls. "I have always viewed children as gods greatest gift. I hope you kissed your girls this morning. Because you might not see them anymore." Tears begin to fall down her eyes. She now believes the rumors about Joe omes to his family. She hears a cell phone ring. She figures Joe has the phone on speaker. She hears Ms Gonzalez voice over the phone are true.

That he is very cold hearted and unmerciful towards people. Especially when it c. "How many times must I tell y'all not to fuck with my family. I have your little spy." Ms Gonzalez start cursing over the phone. "Now that is not nice. Say good by to this gorgeous woman." Then out of nowhere a gunshot and detective Sanchez brains is all over the steering wheel and dashboard. Joe exit the vehicle so does the person with him. He begins to walk towards the courthouse steps. "You always wanted to be in this life now your in it. Your Territory is now mine. My nephew Buckshot will manage it for me. You will get twenty percent I will get the rest. If think about calling your son in Mexico. Think again if I remember correctly he is still wanted by every major federal authorities in this country. Now go see to those orphaned girls they are going to miss their mother."

Joe laughs as he hangs up the phone, he turns to the person walking with him. A muscular man black a person built like Lawrence Taylor. "Make sure Fredric is protected in prison. I take care of my men." He shakes his head and climbs into a waiting Buick Then leaves. Joe climbs into his black Lincoln navigator. "Now representative we're did we leave off before we were interrupted? Next to Joe was a black male in an expensive black suite. With a bald head and a nice watch. His name in Nathaniel Young "My friends in the corrections department said they have to transfer your father to another prison." Joe starts to look angry. Because of all the stuff that has been going on he forgot about his father. He faked his death and had him in prison the last ten years. Under a different name. "People are starting to ask questions." "Move him to one of the prisons here. And please make sure this time you use the name of a person doing life. Not a person on death row."

Said Joe to the representative face. He kept calm and didn't waver. "You must do something about Willcots. I know you heard what he said to the district attorney?" Joe looks at him like a person hearing something for the tenth time. "I already know. It will be dealt with after my brother finishes his investigation." "What about the undercover F.B.I agent I told you about?" "Already taken care of. Plus, your daughter is safe at my house with my daughter." He shakes Joe hand then exit the truck. Then he climbs into a black Buick then leaves.

As the truck begins to leave the man in the passenger seat. Turns around and looks at Joe then says. "We have to deal with him after this is over. He can ruin you and bring you down. Plus he will do anything to keep his job." Joe begins to ponder what his lawyer told him. He knows he is right especially with the current events. He knows it will not be long before someone figure out he is feeding him information. "After my brother's investigation then we will deal with all of our enemies" His lawyer shakes his head in agreement.

CHAPTER 21

Detective Green hangs up the phone and continues to sift through police files looking for answers. He has been searching for about an hour. He keeps asking uniformed officers if they have seen detective Sanchez. She was supposed to be here with him searching these files after she had lunch. He still can't find nothing on Amber and his nice. Plus the rest of the friends. He did put the rest under police protection. Only his nice and the representative daughter refused. Because they are staying with his brother at his house. Which lieutenant Post finds that a bit odd. So he starts investigating there connection.

Detective Green continues to search every police file open and closed to see if there is a connection. As well as reviewing the evidence all over again to see if he missed something. Then out of nowhere a coffee cup is placed in front of him. He turns to his left to see who placed the cup. He noticed that its captain Martinez who is acting more friendlier than usual. "Still looking at old case files trying to find a connection?" "Yes, still nothing. I have been looking for the past three hours." Says detective Green while taking a sip of coffee.

"By the way. Isn't Sanchez suppose to help you?" Green puts down the coffee. Then he begins to ponder on were is she. "She told me she was going to lunch then she would help. Did she give you the file I told her to type?" Martinez looks at Green like he didn't know what he is talking about. "No she told me you was typing it." Immediately Martinez grabs his radio then says very loudly. "I am putting out app out for detective Sanchez. Anyone seeing bring her to HQ ASAP. That is a direct order." He puts the radio on the desk next to detective Green. Then over the radio someone says. "I see her car across the street at the city hall parking lot. 10-13 10-13 offer down officer down." After hearing that everyone in the police department ran outside. By the time Green and Martinez got there. Some of the officers were crying. Some was keeping people back saying. "It's not a pretty site."

Martinez orders the crime scene unit and orders a complete lockdown of the area. After about ten minutes there are a lot of reporters and tv crews. Lieutenant Post arrives on the scene saying. "One of the uniformed officers told me Sanchez was in the video room watching the interrogation." Martinez and Green look at each other then look at Post. "What the hell was she doing there?" Green asked. "She translated from Waterbury police department. I am going to check on why she transferred." Martinez says. "Who okayed her transfer without doing the proper check?" Detective Green asked. "I did it was me." The chief of police says joining Martinez, Post and Green at the crime scene. Martinez orders the crime scene unit and orders a complete lockdown of the area.

"I have to do a report and report this to internal Affairs. You better hope she checks out as a actual police officer not a person impersonating a police officer." Martinez says to the chief. Then a uniformed officer comes to detective Green. "Detective your optometrist says she is ready for you anytime. Answer your dam phone I am not your personal messenger." They all begins to laugh but quietly. Then out of nowhere four black suv pulled up with men in black suits and one female. The female Green recognize as his ex partner's wife. Agent Morales of the F.B.I she approach the men flashing her credentials. " This is now a federal crime scene we are taking over?" Before the chief could say something one of the agents show him a legal document then hand him a cell phone. Then after ten minutes he says. "Everyone clear out its there investigation."

Detective Green tries to talk to the chief but he put his hands up. Green stops then begins to curse to himself. "Don't worry I will find out what is going on. You continue with your investigation and get me that report that Sanchez was supposed to do." Captain Martinez says then walks away. Detective Green walks to his car which is in the police parking lot. Two blocks from the crime scene. "Wait for me detective" someone yells. Green noticed it's lieutenant Post who eventually catches up to him. He is breathing kind of hard. "You need to leave those beers alone." They both start to laugh. Once in the car lieutenant Post asked. We're are we going?" "To my optometrist. Trust me you are going to like her. One more thing don't tell anyone about her." After Green says that he nods yes. But has a confused look on his face. They drive till they get to the Bridgeport library. Lieutenant Post is looking even more confused. They get out of the car and walk through the double door. They bypassed the front desk waving hi to people checking out books. They enter the elevator which is small just enough room for the two of them.

Green pulls out a key which fits into the elevator and the elevator moves up it continues to go up passing the second floor. Lieutenant Post is even more confused because there are only two buttons on the elevator. It stops at a floor which has no number. They both exit the unknown floor. It full of file cabinets old newspaper clippings. Then they hear the sound of a 12 gauge shot gun. They both turn around with their hands in the air. "Ahh lieutenant Post one of the few honest police officer in Bridgeport." The woman with the gun is a middle age white female with long black hair sporting a sexy female suit.

"Going on a date Liz?" Green asked with a smile on his face. "Actually, yes tonight maybe early now since you are early." "Yeah, the feds took over the investigation of the dead officer just now." "I can tell you why follow me gentlemen." They both follow to a computer which has a big screen. You can tell with the three nice size computer screens that this is her office. She begins to type very fast then with in seconds detective Sanchez face appears on the screen but not in a police uniform. She is wearing a nice suit shanking the hand of a average size white male. The logo in the background says F.B.I

They both were taken back by the revaluation. Both Green and lieutenant Post began to start thinking. Before they can say anything, Liz begins to speak. "She graduated from F.B.I academy two years ago. According to report she was planted as a detective in the Waterbury police department. She was undercover in their department. To investigate police corruption. She was doing so well she ended up working for the Gonzalez crime family. They have enough evidence to bust the whole family. But the special agent in charge is so fixated with your brother Joe Dickerson" Detective Green got up started pacing back and forth for two minutes then said. "Who is the special agent in charge that got Detective Sanchez killed?" "Agent Morales. Your old partner wife is the agent in charge. Like I said earlier she has enough evidence to bust the Gonzalez family but not your brother. Your brother has possible deniability. In english he is clean." Detective Green sat down and put his hands in his face. Lieutenant Post pats him on the back. "I will take care of this detective. Give me the complete file so I can give it to my friend on news 12." Green lifts his head up and turns towards Post. He shakes his head in approval. Liz hands Post a thick file before she can say anything Post says.

"This never came from you. You have my word." She begins to smile in approval. "Now detective Green hear is what you really came here for. It took me awhile to find anything, but I eventually find something. You brother went to great lengths to cover this up. You might remember this incident, Lieutenant." She pulls up an old newspaper clipping of a girl that drowned at a pool at the YMCA. The look on Post face was a look of surprise. "I remember that. I was a sergeant at the time. A police detective daughter drowned at the pool. According to witnesses she was pushed into the pool. By the girls that was bullying her."

Liz blew up the picture on the newspaper clippings. "You might recognize the people in the clippings detective Green." Detective Green did recognize the people in the clippings. Two of the girls are murder victims the other three has not been killed yet. He also recognize one of the police officers in uniform. Which is his old partner. "Who is the daughter's father?" "Detective Isaac Pond" Liz says. "I know detective Pond very good detective the best in the state." Post said. "We're is Pond now?" Asked Green. "That is a mystery. For some reason he left the force after all five girls were never prosecuted. He joined the department of Corrections for NYPD. His brother is the head man in charge. He was doing a routine inspection of Sing Sing Prison were he disappeared.

There is no police file of the incident at the YMCA nor is there anymore news coverage of it." "Why is that?" Post asked. "Joe owns the newspaper company through a shell company. So any bad press about him he is quashed immediately." "Where is the reporter who post the news about the YMCA incident." Detective Green asked "He also disappeared there is still a missing person report on him. He is the funny thing though. Joe filed the missing person report." "Which means he is looking for him." Post says with a smile on his face he turns to Green who also has the same smile. They both are thinking the same thing. "Before we try to find the reporter we need to go to Boston and question Johnathan Morales. My old partner he was first on the scene he can tell us something" Lieutenant Post agrees with him. Then he showed him the file he was given. Singling he has to make a quick stop before the long drive.

They thank Liz and take the elevator down to the first floor while walking to the car lieutenant Post was on the phone he talked for about ten minutes then says to detective Green. "We need to stay here for five minutes so I can give this to my reporter friend" after five minutes a black BMW pulls up and Post handed the person in the BMW the report then the reporter drove off.

CHAPTER 22

Detective Green and Lieutenant Post exit the train at the Boston south street station. It's just as busy as Grand central in New York. Lots of college kids some everyday people going about. It's six pm at night so this is the rush hour crowd going home. Green looks at his watch then looks at Post who shakes his head no. "We are not going to the Red Sox playoff game." Green begins to laugh because Post is a Yankee Fan and they didn't. Make the playoff. They walk till they get to were all the cabs are located.

Before Post can wave for a cab someone yells out. "Detective Green over here." Both Post and Green look to see who it is. It's two uniformed Boston Police officers. They walk towards the officers. Two white males one with a bald head the other with a basic crew cut. "Do you need a ride somewhere detective? We recognize you from the pictures of Sargent Morales." "That is who we came to see officers. I am Lieutenant Post." Post extended his hand. "I am officer Hines and this is officer Duffy. We will take to the the Sargent. He is with the captain at HQ for the press conference." Both Green and post smile in approval.

They see how Morales got better by leaving Bridgeport Police. They see how he was able to flex more. Plus they see how Bridgeport police was holding him back. They remains quiet the whole ride. The two officers radio in that they are here to see Morales. They exit the police car in front of the police headquarters in Boston. They begin to walk to the entrance. They see a lot of reporters exiting the building. One of them recognize detective Green then almost immediately runs to Green saying. "Detective Green is Morales connected to the murders in Bridgeport."

After that reporter said that he was surrounded in seconds by reporters. Green and Lieutenant Post was escorted in by uniformed officers. Green gives Post that sorrowful look. Post gives him a reassurance smile. They are now in the building and is met by

Morales who still has the scar from the flash bank that blew up in his face. He lost some weight. Plus, he is now sporting expensive suite. Green and morales give each other a huge hug. "Let me guess I am connected to those two high profile murders in Bridgeport?" Both Green and Post shake there heads yes. "Use my office." Says a big white male in plane cloths. "Detective Morales and Lieutenant Post this is commissioner Jim Skye." Jim shakes both Green and Post hand. Green has heard of commissioner Skye he was heavily criticized for hiring Morales. People thinking he will bring Bridgeports problems to Boston. In the past two years he has proved that hiring Morales was the right thing.

They take the elevator to the top floor. When they entered the commissioner's office they see pictures of past commissioner's awards statues. Post and Green admire the excellent view of Boston. Green knows this is a intimidation tactic. "My brothers office in Stamford has this same type of view. I am going to tell you what I told him I don't scare that easily and stop overcompensating." The commissioner has a frown on his face after what Green said. They all sit on the conference table in the office. "What do you remember of the drowning of that girl at the YMCA pool six years ago?"

Morales has a look of surprise on his face so does the commissioner. "Everything I know is in the police report." "That report is missing. We can't find it know were. It's almost like it never happened if it wasn't for a old newspaper clip everyone forgot about." Detective Green cut in "I typed my report and gave it to at the time Lieutenant Martinez." "Who is now captain Martinez." Post cut in. "Why give it to Martinez?" Green asked. "He ordered me and every officer on the scene to give him their report. He ordered us to I handcuffs the five girls we arrested. One girl father is a respected Judge. The other worked in Hartford legislature Plus your brother was there Green."

Green slams his fist on the table. "My brother covered this up he used this incident to gain very powerful people in his pocket." "That is how he got so much power in Bridgeport and in Connecticut." Post cut in. "If your going to bring him down it's going to be a struggle because he has people in the legislature In his pocket." The commissioner says. "They know we came here thanks to the reporters. You need to put a protective detail on Morales." Post said the commissioner nods in agreement. "Following me to my office and

I will give you my police notes. I never turned them in it should help." They all got up and exit the commissioner office. They followed him into the elevator to the fourth floor to a door that says Homicide task force. Once in the room there are six desk a huge touch screen monitor on the wall on one of the walls were photos of criminals they caught. They went into a office that read squad commander. Detective Green is feeling happy seeing how Morales is doing so well in just two years. He knows now that there is life outside of the Bridgeport police department. The office is full of newspapers clippings that are framed. Pictures of his family and other detective in the squad. "You are doing so well. I can't wait to tell everyone in Bridgeport on how well you are doing." Green said while admiring one of the newspapers clippings.

"No need chief Gill Ridges came here last year to try to recruit me back. He was shocked when he saw I was the squad commander. He walked out with his head down." Morales says then everyone breaks out in laughter. "If you ever want to transfer to Boston let me know." "He is staying right in Bridgeport Morales." Lieutenant Post cut in stopping detective Green from answering. Morales goes into his desk and hands Green a black notebook. "The newspapers reporter who did the story is in hiding. His wife filed a missing person report. He is still missing to this day. Talk to my wife she used to work missing person unit in the F.B.I. She worked the case she may be able to tell you about him."

Green and Post thanked Morales while they walked out of the door. They took the elevator to the first floor lobby were they are met by the two officers who brought them. "We were told to give you a ride to the train station. They got into the car and headed to the train station.

CHAPTER 23

Green and lieutenant Post enter the Amtrak train. They went to the business car of the train. They sat in the back with lieutenant Post sitting across from Green. "So you're the reason we were told to hold the train. Now we can leave." Says the train conductor with a smile on his face. Green looks at Post both thinking the same thing. "They really wanted us out of Boston." Post says "You can't blame them Bridgeport has a bad reputation." Post agrees with Green but he keeps it to himself. He knows how corrupt the city is from the head down. Despite all the arrest all the good he has done. Green opens the the note book and he goes to the day of the YMCA drowning.

Detective Green continues to read the notebook. He comes upon three names that Morales wrote down that he noted as witness. "There are three witnesses to the drowning a Joe Davis, William Devlin, and Ronald Rackham. According to Morales they witness the drowning. The girls bullied her pushed her into the pool. My niece tried to jump in and save her, but the other girls stopped her saying she is fat she will float." Lieutenant Post put his hands in front of his face then slapped them on the table. Reacting what detective Green read from the notebook. Your brother and the other girls we are protecting is guilty of murder. Their parents cover up a murder."

Green nods his head yes. Lieutenant Post pulls out his phone and begins talking to someone. Green can tell it is one of his detective from his unit. He talked for ten minutes then hangs up the phone. "I got one of my detective looking for those names right now. Hopefully when we get to Bridgeport he will have the location. Also the F.B.I has arrested Ms Gonzalez and the rest of her organization. My leak to the press paid off." They both smiled and detective Green continues to read the note book. Detective Green read the note book for about ten more minutes. When he yell out. "There we're cameras in the building. Facing the pool." Everyone on the train tuned and looked at them. Post smiled then looked at Green and said. "Calm down what do you mean cameras?" "There are cameras facing the pool. According to Morales he wrote down that he went to retrieve the tapes but they were missing." "Who was doing security that day?" Post asked.

"A Jerry Sumner." "We need to have a chat with Mr Sumner." Post makes a phone call on his cell phone he talked on his phone for about ten minutes. Then he hangs up. "Jerry Sumner died six months after the YMCA incident. His wife found him dead with his throat slit. According the the police report the house was a mess. Like someone was looking for something." Detective Green begins staring at the table like a person in deep thought. "What if the reporter got the tapes? Jerry could have sold them to the reporter for a lot of money." After detective Green said that lieutenant Post picks up his phone again. Talks for another ten minutes then says. "We will know once we reach Bridgeport. Also trust me I am using men from my unit. That is who I have been calling. I gave them strict instructions not to use police computers. Between me and you I do not trust captain Martinez."

Detective Green agrees with lieutenant Post. As of right now he can't be trusted. Post leave's to grab then something to eat from the dining car. Green puts the notebook down and begins to stare at the window. The one thing Green likes about taking the train is seeing all the wonderful scenery. Whizzing By and the time to think on things. Lieutenant Post comes back without Green ever noticing. Puts a cup of coffee in front of him. The coffee is Hazelnut Green can tell from the smell of it. "Try to relax before we get to Bridgeport. This is the only time you will probably be able to." Lieutenant Post says while drinking coffee.

Green begin to until the face of the two dead girls keep popping up in his head. Green begins to feel sorry for them. He feels they didn't deserve to die like they did. Even though this may be their past coming back to harm them. Green drinks his coffee and starts to enjoy the scenery.

Chapter 24

The train arrived at Bridgeport train station. Detective Green and Lieutenant Post exit the train. Not a lot of people exit the train. Bridgeport is not a desirable place for people to visit. With the high crime and bad reputation, the city has. Once they exit, they are met by two men in suits. White males average looking typical F.B.I agents. "Lieutenant Post, detective Green we need you to come with us." The agents say while flashing their F.B.I badge. "What do you want us for? We are busy with an active investigation." Post says in a commanding tone. "You are wanted for interfering with a federal investigation." They recognize the voice of the person who said that. It was agent Morales.

Green old partners wife. "I need both of you to come to the federal building to answer some questions." Both Green and Post notice that she is very upset and angry. Green knows why that is but he is keeping his mouth shut. This could not be the reason they are wanted. Until he finds out why he told himself he will not say anything. Green sees Post has the same expressions on his face. They enter the federal sedan which are all black with Black tented windows. The federal building is not that far from the train station. It is only about three block. They arrive at the federal building. They are escorted into the building and to the six floor.

They are put into separate interrogation rooms. Green is seated for about ten minutes until agent Morales appears. She slams a file on her table. A pretty thin file. "Why are you investigating the disappearance of Stephen Hale?" After she said that Green begins to laugh. Now he begins to realize what is going. Someone is using the F.B.I to get information on Stephen so they can find him. "You said we were?" "You don't ask me question detective I do." "Not when you are getting false information and someone wants to use that information to kill someone." After Green said that he can tell she is beginning to start thinking. She gets up and slams the door immediately. Detective Green sits in the interrogation room for about twenty minutes until a man in a suit says. "You can go sorry for the inconvenience. You can get your gun at the front desk."

Green gets up and leaves. He sees lieutenant Post leaves at the same time. They collect their guns then walk outside of the federal building. We're they are met by one of the detective in lieutenant Post squad. "What's up Rock." Green laughing while saying it. "You know I hate when you call me that. I found the missing reporter's wife. She went back using her maiden name. That is what made it difficult to track her down." "Did you use the department computer to find her?" Post ask. "Hell no I use the old fashioned method I looked for her." Both Green and Post nod their heads in agreement.

They drove till they reached Trumbull they pass the entrance to get on the highway till they reached a apartment complex but it is designed as a condominium with each unit has a first floor and second floor. Green and lieutenant Post exit the car and head towards the door. They knock on the door a couple of times. Till someone answer. "Hello who is it." She opens the door Green sees this middle age white female. Who reminds him of Vana White from wheel of fortune. "I know who you are detective ,lieutenant come inside so we can talk."

They step into her condo which is beautiful inside full of pictures of her husband plus awards he has won as a reporter. "My husband has dedicated himself to report the truth. It pains me to see that he is missing because of your brother detective Green. I know you can't control what he does but he is a cancer on this city." She is crying while speaking. Green can sense the hatred she has for his family, and he can't blame her. "I know why you both are here detective. You want the security tapes. Please stay right hear? Both Green and lieutenant Post is shocked. They stay seated while she went up stairs.

She comes downstairs with a set of keys. She then walks to to the hall closet on the first floor. She opens a false bottom and pulls out three VHS tapes marked YMCA pool security tapes. She hands them to detective Green. "Don't let my husband die in vain." She says while handing the tapes to detective Green. "I thought you said he was missing?" Lieutenant Post said. "I have to see if I can trust you both now I can let me show you something." She leaves to go to the kitchen. She comes back two minutes later with a package of ground meat with a message saying. We're are the tapes. Green and Post have a shocking reaction. Then Green says. "We are looking at her husband.

We need the F.B.I to analyze this." Detective Green leaves to get gloves from the car. He put the Ground meat in an evidence bag. While lieutenant Post is on the phone. "The F.B.I is on the way to pick this up let's meet them outside. They shake her hand and make a promise to her to find the killer. They begin to walk to the car when detective Green felt a burning sensation. In his right shoulder. He new he has been shot. He immediately turns and dives for cover. Lieutenant Post begins to return fire.

Which is coming from two black suv. "This is lieutenant Post we have a 10-13 officer down I repeat 10-13 officer down. We need backup now." Lieutenant Post yelled while trying to duck bullets and shattered glass from cars hit with gun fire. "I am sorry lieutenant backup is not available. I repeat backup is not available." Says the 911 operator. Then out of know where someone was returning fire. Post recognize that it's the F.B.I who is assisting them. Three of the shooters are dead one is alive by surrendering.

One of the agents came towards lieutenant Post and grabs his radio. "This is agent Morales of the F.B.I consider your whole department under federal investigation. For abandoning your men." She gives lieutenant Post back his radio then says. "Are you okay?"

CHAPTER 25

Joe sits down at his favorite Italian restaurant eating steak. In the VIP room of the restaurant at downtown Bridgeport. He is interrupted by his lawyer Michael Vintoro and his friend Michael Ferally. "We have a problem." Ferally says while sitting across from Joe at the table. A waiter came and poured Mr. Ferally some wine. He also poured Mr. Vintoro some wine also. Who is sitting just with in arm length of Joe. Joe stops eating and wipes his lips with a napkin. He begins to Sigh in frustration. "What is it this time?" Joe says while rolling his eyes. Both Vintoro and Ferally look at each other.

"You really don't know?" Ferally says with concern. "I told my father you had nothing to do with this. Don't worry we got your back. Who ever did this is going to pay." After Mr. Ferally said that he got up and made a phone call on his cell phone. Joe slammed his hand on the table then says. "What the fuck is going on." "Your brother was just shot. While interviewing a witness. He took a round in the shoulder. Somebody ordered backup not to come. It had the looks of a well coordinated attack." After Vintoro said that the look on Joe's face put fear in both mens eyes.

Mr. Ferally finishes his phone call after being on it for ten minutes. "My father said he has your back. Your brother is helping us out. Weather he knows it or not. We need to find out who is killing people in our and your organizations." "Don't you mean mine. I am the one paying these men. Plus keeping them safe. You and your father has benefited and y'all have not helped one bit." After Joe said that there's an awkward silence for five minutes. "Joe how about me and you go to Bridgeport Hospital to see your brother. Mr. Ferally I will keep you posted." Vintoro and Joe leave the restaurant and hop in the waiting black SUVs.f

"Driver take us to Bridgeport Hospital. You shouldn't have said that to him. You know him and his father is looking for a reason to take you out." Joe continue to sit in silence with a look that can kill. Joe trying his best to ignore Vintoro. So he can figure out who did this. "Contact our person in the police department. Ask if they caught any of the shooters. Also don't tell me what I can say and can't say. Plus let them try to take me out and please remain silent I need to think." They stay silent the all the way to the hospital.

CHAPTER 26

Lieutenant Post looks at detective Green. Who is in the hospital bed hooked up to the telemetry. Green just came back from surgery to remove the bullet that was in his right shoulder. Post mad at himself for not seeing this coming. Also mad that back up refused to come and help. He is also worried about Green's girlfriend who went into labor after hearing that Green was shot. Post immediately turns to his right to see who is coming into the room. He immediately grabs his gun. After see who is coming in. It's Green's brother Joe.

The chief of police stops lieutenant Post then says. "He has been cleared he didn't order the hit on you and Green. He has an alibi." "This is not your call chief. This is a F.B.I investigation." Post cut in while still holding the gun. "Not anymore. Internal Affairs is taking over. F.B.I is out of there jurisdiction. That reminds me they are looking for you so they can get your statement." Post lowers his gun and walks past Joe who has a smile on his face. Joe walks up to detective Green who is still sleeping . He hears the door close behind him. He pulls out a gun he takes the safety off.

He then place the gun under the pillow. He sees his brother move a little but didn't wake up. Joe figured he still must be under the anesthesia. He then says to his brother. "I know you can hear me bro. There is a gun under your pillow. I will find out who did this and they will pay. Your girlfriend had the baby. It's a girl a baby girl. Don't worry I will keep them safe. Rest up bro." He wipes the tears from his eyes. He walks towards the door to leave. He steps into the hallway of the Intensive care unit. Which is full of police officers. A nurse walks pas him and is heading to his brother room. Joe is approached by a Hispanic woman in a gorgeous suit. He recognized the woman as special agent Morales of the F.B.I the wife of his brother former partner. "You know who I am Joe we need to ask you some questions concerning the death of newspaper reporter Christian Thompson." After she said that two shots rang out from detective Green's room. Everyone runs into detective Green's room. They see the nurse on the floor. With a gunshot wound in the left shoulder. Next to her right hand in a loaded gun. Joe infuriated with anger. Shoves the police officers aside.

Grabs the women then yell's. "Who hired you to kill my brother." "She told me to. She said if I do this I wont go to jail." "Who is she?" Joe yells while the police officers stand aside and let him question the nurse. "His girlfriend the police officer Ashley." After she said that everyone except Joe and a few police officers ran to the maternity ward. The officers that remained took the nurse into custody. They escort her with other doctors so she can get her gunshot wounds looked at. "Make sure you read her. Her Miranda rights. How did detective Green get a gun? Lieutenant Post is supposed to be holding it." Said the chief of police.

"I gave him the gun. I figured who ever hired those guys may try again." Joe said to the chief of police. "If you plan on arresting my client think twice. Not a jury in the world would convict him." Joe's lawyer said. "No we are not." The chief said as he talks to lieutenant Post. "Give my client some time agent Morales. As you can see." She put up her hand as to cut him off. "I will wait for you right here or we can use the conference room on this floor." Agent Morales walks away. Joe walks to the bathroom with his lawyer. They check to make sure they are alone. "I already know what you are going to say.

I will put things into motion." The lawyer said. Then a knock came on the door. Then in walks Joe's driver. "They lost her Ashley escape the hospital." "Thanks wait for me at the car." "I will put all our resources to finding her." "Put a huge bounty out for. I want her alive." Joe says in a menacing tone. They both leave the bathroom and try to find the doctor to get a update. The lawyer begins to talk on the phone. While at the nurse charge station he feels a tap on his shoulder. Joe turns around to see who it is. "Thanks for saving detective Green's life. Now I already know you know Ashley escape.

Don't go looking for her. Stay out of this." Lieutenant Post says. Joe smiles then walks away. Lieutenant Post walks towards detective Green. "If you are up to it Dr. Chen wants to talk to us. He is in the morgue right now." Green nods his head yes. He sits on the side of the bed trying to get his bearings. Green still feels a little groggy. He takes his time getting up. He stumbles a little but is able to get his balance. He grabs his clothes from the closet and walks in the bathroom to get dress. He was able to get dress while his left arm in the sling. Because of the gunshot wound in his left shoulder. The doctor comes in the room.

Hands detective green his discharge papers. The he turns to the lieutenant and says. "How long will this room be shutdown?" "For awhile because this is a crime scene." "I have friends in the mayor's office. We will see about this." He storms out. Lieutenant Post and detective Green leave the intensive care unit

CHAPTER 27

Joe walks towards the the conference room which is located down the hall. As he is walking people are moving aside like he is some king. He comes to the conference room. The door to the room is not see through. Which means you can have sensitive meetings in here. Plus a lot of privacy. He enters the room. He sees his lawyer and agent Morales sitting down talking. Morales gets up walks towards Joe then says. "looks like we don't need to talk to you. Someone came forward and confessed." She leaves like a scornful woman. The door closes then Joe says to his lawyer. "What is going on?" With the look of confusion on his face.

"You may not like this Joe. Just remember he volunteered." "Who volunteered? Spit it the fuck out." Joe said so loudly people we knocking on the door asking if everything is ok. The lawyer goes to assure everything is okay. He comes back. Then says to Joe. "It was Fredric who confessed. He took the charge so you will be clean." After hearing that Joe begins to pace back and forth. Anger begins to swell with in him. "This would have never happened if David did what I told him." Joe said while staring at the conference room table. His lawyer is now the one with a confused look.

"David was supposed to get rid of the body. So I guess that dumb fuck chopped his body up and gave it to his wife." "I will see to it he is brought to you immediately." After the lawyer said that. They begin to head to the door. "Wait. Make sure Fredric's family is taking care of. Anything they need we will help them. Also make sure Fredric is sent to a prison in this state that we control. He can help us make more money on that end." They head for the door and exit the conference room. They continue till they get to the black suv were the driver is outside the car. The driver motions himself to Joe then says.

"They have found Ashley. She was caught in her old neighborhood. Our people is holding her in the building we own in New Era Court.

CHAPTER 28

Lieutenant Post and detective Green is met with security. Upon reaching the basement of Bridgeport Hospital. The security guard who is armed recognize lieutenant Post and Green. The security guard is a former police officer. Who retired this year because of all the protests. He was in his 25th year. So he retired with full pension. A white male average built. "I already know why you are here. The Dr sent me to escort you to the medical examiner wing." Post and Green nodded in approval. They follow him down the dark corridor. Lieutenant Post is shocked and amazed that they are under the street. He didn't know these tunnels we're here.

"How long was has these tunnels been here?" Post asked. "These been here for a long time. These tunnels are small compared to the ones under Yale New Haven Hospital." Post is shocked by what the security guard said. They walk for a good five minutes. Till they reach a door that said Medical Examiner's. He used his badge to open the metal doors. Detective Green knows why the extra security was added. When the entered the room they hear Jazz music playing. Lieutenant Post paused to appreciate the music that is playing. They see Dr. Chen in his office talking on the phone.

While other we're doing a autopsy on a body. They walk to Chen's office. Who motions them to sit in the two chairs in his office. He has his many degrees on the wall. Pictures of him on vacation. Plus framed newspaper clippings. Detective Green notice a military medal on his desk. He talks on the phone for another ten minutes then he hangs up the phone. "Sorry guy's I was on the phone with my daughter. We have to wait for someone else." Both Post and Green feels confused. Both begin to wonder who else is coming? Who else want the autopsy results. Chen's office door open and in walks agent Morales. Lieutenant Post begins to say.

"Who called her? This is a police investigation. We don't believe yet that this case is connected." Post said sternly with conviction. "Yes it does if you don't mind me explaining Lieutenant." Dr. Chen respond in a calmly tone. Agent Morales takes a seat next to Chen's desk. "All the victims died of Curare. It is a form of poison if injected it is fatal." The look on agent Morales tells she had heard of this poison before. "This particular poison is very fatal. There is no cure it kills the victim very fast." Dr. Chen nodded his head in agreement on what Morales just said. "It comes from a plant found in South America.

It is used by the cartel's a lot down there." "The plant is found in several Botanical Gardens in New York." Dr. Chen finishes. "But who would have the skills to make this poison and put it in a device that is so undetectable?" Lieutenant Post asked. "You ever heard back from New York department of corrections on detective Pond" Green asked. "I did some background check on detective Pond." Chen cut in "He has military experience he is a former Marine." After Dr. Chen said that the room got quiet. Then after five minutes Green begin to say.

"If nobody going to say it I will former police detective Pond is the killer. All of our victims so far are connected to the death of his daughter. Who obviously didn't get justice." "If that is the case your case and mind are connected." Morale cut in. "But detective Pond didn't kill the reporter. Who ever covered up the death of the reporter did." Detective Green said. Agent Morales slams her hand on the desk in frustration. Then she said. "My part in this case ends then. Because Fredric confessed for the murder of the reporter." "That is a lie. He is taking the fall for someone." Detective Green said loudly. Lieutenant Post taps him on the shoulder to calm him down.

"You should check in on the police details you have on the other potential victims." Morales said as she leaves. Lieutenant Post pulls out his phone to make phone calls. Green knows were Morales is going. It will be hard to get Fredric to flip. "I have a friend in the New York police department who can check the gardens plus the correctional facility." Green nodded in agreement on Chen proposal for help. Chen begins making phone call on his phone. Lieutenant Post spent several minutes on the phone then he said after he hangs up the phone. "We have another victim."

CHAPTER 29

They arrived in New Era Court from the Central Avenue entrance. This place use to be nice. Joe still remembers a time when he would come here to hangout with his friends. That was back when this place was good to look upon. Beautiful town houses two blocks from a major park and right on the bus line. Now it's a eye sore. Nothing but drunks and crackheads. They reach the last town house were. Was two men in dark clothes standing next to the door. Joe gets out of the truck. "We got her inside. Don't worry we have the building sound proof."

Joe walks in with a smile on his face. His lawyer trailing behind him. They see Ashley tied up in a chair with the look of fear on her face. Joe walks closer to her with anger building up in him. He sees a metal pipe on the table in the room. Which if residents was living here it would be a living room. Joe points to the metal pipe. One of the two men in the room grabs the pipe and hands it to him. Ashley begins to beg for her life. Joe feels a tap on his shoulder. He knows it is his lawyer. "Who has hired you to kill my clients brother?" "If I tell you will you let me live? I promise I will disappear. Me and my baby."

Ashley replied while tears coming down her eyes. Joe tighten his grip on the metal pipe. His anger building even more with her attempt to bargain. "You have nothing to bargain with. You are wanted for conspiracy and attempting murder of a police detective. You are done. Now tell us who hired you?" Joe lawyer said. Then Joe slams the metal pipe on the ground next to Ashley. Scaring her so much she begins to talk. "David hired me your nephew David Buckshot." After she said that out of nowhere Joe begins to hit her savagely with the metal pipe. Everyone in the room was so scared seeing Joe reaction. His lawyer went to one of the men in the room. "Find David and bring him here." "No problem I know were he is." The men left the Town House to find David.

Joe and his lawyer are in the room for 15 minutes before they arrived with David. When they bring him in he immediately is caught off guard and fear begins to come over him. "You lied to me. You said my uncle wanted to congratulate me?" David hands start to shake. He is so scared he can't hear anything anybody is saying. The lifeless body of Ashley has him in so much fear. She is beaten so bad she is unrecognizable. Plus there is so much blood on the floor is like a small pool. Then his uncle Joe is covered head to toe in blood. Joe immediately picks up the metal pipe. Then hits David in the knee cap to get his attention.

David is on the ground screaming in pain. "We know you hired ashley to kill your uncle while he was in the hospital. Did you order the hit on him that sent him to the hospital?" The lawyer asked while David was crying in pain. Joe standing above him with the metal pipe in his hand. David then scream out. "I was hired by the Italians but they are mad because I acted too early." After he said this Joe looks at his lawyer. With the look of shock on his face. While his lawyer had a different look on his face. Like he somewhat suspected this. Joe and his lawyer walk to the corner of the room. The part that didn't have a lot of blood on the floor.

"They probably wanted him dead in the beginning. But because of the killings you're brother became a asset. They want to use this to the people we have on our pockets. To be in their pocket." Joe agree with his lawyer. "Set a meeting with the Judge and the representative. Let's show them who is in charge. I am going up stairs to take a shower. Take care of this." Joe starts to head up stairs when on of the men said. "What do you want us to do with this peace of shit." They said while pointing at David. "Kill him save me the head. Put it in a cooler with ice for me." They started laughing in agreement with Joe. David start to scream in fear. Then he starts to talking about other things. The lawyer stopped them to let David talk.

The lawyer sits in the truck waiting for Joe. Joe finally walked in the truck. I set up the meeting. The men are cleaning up the town house. The representative Is going to be late to the meeting. Because his daughter is dead. She is the next victim. Your brother is on the scene. They have a suspect. I hope your ready for this." Joe continues to remain silent while he process everything.

CHAPTER 30

Lieutenant Post and detective Green arrive at the crime scene. Which is located on 879 Gilman ST. Which is not far from Saint Mary's by the sea. A place we're everyone in Bridgeport goes to see the fire works. Beautiful place to go for a walk our enjoy the rise and fall of the sun. Now this place is full of police officers and citizens with their cellphone out recording. Detective Green already notice at least five news reporter trucks. As soon as Post and Green exit the vehicle. They are swarmed with reporters and citizens with cell phone. Three police officers escorted them to the crime scene while saying. "No comment" they finally get through.

Then detective Green tells the officers. Move the crime scene tape back another five feet." They nodded in agreement and begin to do so. They finally come upon the house. It is a ordinary looking out. Grass is unkept but the house look like it was just painted recently. Both Post and Green stopped to look at the house. "I know. The house doesn't look like a place someone who represents Bridgeport in Hartford would live in." Green recognizes the person immediately as one of Post men. "Nathaniel's daughter comes here when she don't want to stay. In the Dorm at Fairfield University." The strange thing is only four people know about this place. The father, mother, Joe and Joe's daughter."

After the detective finished talking Green tries to figure out who else new. He leaves them and starts walking around analyzing the crime scene. He walks pass several forensic officers. Who are collecting evidence, and trying to find fingerprints. He walks into the house we're he runs into more forensic officers. He also run into the chief of police. Who notice detective Green almost immediately. He walks towards him. "You should be at the hospital with your newborn baby. Plus you aren't cleared by medical to be back in the field." "I am fine plus my sister in law is with my daughter. What are you doing to find Ashley?" Green said sternly. "We are still looking for her. We have a city wide bulletin out on her." "That's not enough. Hello chief we are taking over this investigation." Agent Morales says while handing the chief a letter. He immediately turns red with anger and storms out. "You are still on this case if you want to detective." Green nods yes. "I already sent agents to New York. The governor wanted us to take over since the representative daughter is dead." Green watches while agent Morales barks orders.

Green continues to look around analyzing the scene. He looks at the door with one of the forensic officers. "No damage to the lock at all. The killer might have had a key to the place." After he heard this Green is left with more questions than answers. Lieutenant Post calls detective Green outside. "I already know about the F.B.I taking over." "That is not why I called you over. One of the neighbors noticed a painting crew here two weeks ago." Green immediately walks to a black suv and knocks on the window. Then window rolls down reveling the representative and his wife. He is holding her while she is in tears.

"Yes detective what do you want? Can you see we are grieving here." "Did you have anything done on the house? This is very important." "Yes I paid to have the house painted." The wife said. Detective Green shows her a picture of detective Pond. "Yes he was one of the painters. Is that who killed my daughter?" "This is a ongoing investigation mam." Agent Morales said while standing behind Green. The both walk away from the suv. "Now we know how he got in. He made copies of the keys and camped out in the house till she showed up." Morale agreed with what Green said. They meet up with lieutenant Post. "We need to get Ramos and Mathew now." "I have agents picking them up now. We are putting them in a undisclosed location."

Morales walks away barking orders on the phone. Green turns to lieutenant Post. "Pond is doing this because he never got justice for his daughter. I need to speak with the nun." One uniformed officers came to lieutenant Post and detective Green. "Green fire chief Zigway wants to see you." Green and lieutenant Post puzzled by the request. Green and Post continue to question neighbors. Then they get back in the car.

CHAPTER 31

Joe and his lawyer pulls into the Italian restaurant on Madison Avenue. It is a beautiful restaurant in the gorgeous part of Bridgeport. The restaurant use to be on the lower part of Madison Avenue. But when this lot became available it moved with no problem. The restaurant also serves as one of the main hangout out for the leader of the Ferally family. Which have connections to other mafia families in New York. The Ferally family use to control Bridgeport but lost to the Dickerson family. The Ferally family became outcast. The other New York families didn't want nothing to do with them. Because they lost control of Bridgeport to a black gang.

At this time of the day the restaurant is pack with the dinner rush. They pull in front of the restaurant the men at the door. You valet park the cars. Open the door. Joe notified them he is not staying long. Joe and his lawyer walks in the restaurant with Joe holding a cooler. The place is pack with a lot of people. There's a long line of people waiting to be seated. With them yelling at the hostess saying. "We made reservations." There's beautiful painting on the wall. Of places in Italy. Joe all ways hated coming here because of the way blacks, and Hispanic are treated here.

Plus the cooks in the back are not Italian but Mexican. Who are not allowed to come in the front but only in the back. Joe scans the restaurant for Michael Ferally who is head of the family. He finds him talking to the mayor of Bridgeport and New Haven. Joe looks to his lawyer. "I will make a mental note. Plus I will set a meeting. New Haven will be yours." The lawyer said. Then out of nowhere someone yell's. "What the fuck." Everyone in the restaurant stop what they are doing. Joe walks in a fast pace to where Michael is at. He throws the cooler on the table. The head of David Buckshot comes out. Everyone starts to scream. Some people vomit.

People start to exit the restaurant. Michael motions Joe to the back room. While barking orders to his men. Tony Michael's son follow his father, Joe and the lawyer to the back room. They walk through the kitchen which is full of Mexicans cooking Italian food. They continue to a walk-in freezer then to a hidden door. Which leads to a office. There's a mini bar, pool table. Various pictures on the wall. The red paint on the walls match the carpet on the floor. They reach his desk then he begins to say. "What in the hell are you doing dropping the head of a dead man on my table?" "The head is my nephew. Who was working with your son. To kill my brother." Joe said loudly.

After hearing this Michael has a look like he doesn't know what is going on. Joe begins to laugh then says. "You didn't know. So your son this this with out you knowing."Michael looks at Tony with such hatred and anger. "I will deal with you later." Michael said to Tony while pointing at him. "Let me fix this Joe. My son was out of line." Joe interrupts him by slamming his hands on the desk. "You know my family is out of bounds." Joe said very loudly and in such a commanding tone. "Since my brother is not dead. I will not go to the commission and ask for your son's life. Here is what I require. You will give me 75% of all your take effective immediately." Joe and his lawyer walks out of the hidden room.

Leaving Michael and Tony by themselves. Once they leave Tony can feel the tension in the room. He sees the look on his face. He has seen it plenty of times. Especially when he screwed up. Tony continues to stare straight ahead. He can feel his father looking at him. He can even feel his breath breathing on the side of his neck. He does this for three more minutes. "What did I tell you?" Michael asked Tony. Tony didn't answer for fear of reprisals. "I told you don't do anything till I tell you to. Plus I told you using that idiot is not a good plan. Because of you we are going to lose a lot of money and you better hope the commission don't find out." Then out of nowhere one of Michael's men came rushing in.

"The representative daughter is dead. Plus detective Green and lieutenant Post may have a suspect." Michael immediately usher Tony out of the room. He walks out in such anger. Soon as the door slams he motion the man to continue. "Remember the girl that drowned six years ago. At the YMCA that Joe covered up." Michael nodded in agreement the whole time the man spoke. "It's her father they are looking for." Michael begins to laugh. Like a man in a happy mood. "We sit back and do nothing. Looks like Joe's past came back to haunt him." Michael says with a huge smile. "There is just one thing." The smile fade immediately after the man spoke. "The way he is killing his victims is like he knows who covered it up." Michael stands looking at while thinking. "There is a shadow player. Follow the detective learn as much as you can. Plus tell everyone my son is no longer involved in family business." The man left immediately.

CHAPTER 32

Detective Green and lieutenant Post pulls up to the Firefighters headquarters on Congress st. They see several firefighters cleaning the fire trucks. They all have shirts on that says firefighter cadet. Lieutenant Post exit the car then walk around to open the door for Green. Green scream a little in pain when his left shoulder hits the door. "You need to go back to the hospital. Let me and my unit take over the case." Post says with some concern in his voice. Green shrugged him off. They continue to the entrance of the firehouse.

They hear music playing some hard rock. They also smell food. They walk to the front desk we're a civilian is at the desk. An older black women who is sipping here coffee. "Detective Green the fire chief is expecting you. Go ahead and take the elevator to the fourth floor." They turn to their left and head to the elevator. They take the elevator to the fourth floor. The door open they continue down the hall. Passing several pictures of the fire chief that is hanging on the wall. They knock on the door. They hear a voice that said. "Please come in."

The enter the room we're they see the mayor of Bridgeport. An average height white male who is trying to run for re-election. "Hello mr mayor." Lieutenant Post said as they walked in. "Hello gentleman. I just dropped by to try to convince your stepfather Green to stay in Bridgeport. He was offered a job with the Baltimore fire department. They want him to run it." Detective Green is shocked but not surprised. The mayor leaves and lieutenant Post and Green sit in the pair of chairs in front of the desk.

"How are doing? Green I want you to return to the hospital. I can tell you are in a lot of pain." Chief Zigway says with some concern. "Why did you call us here?" Green replied. "To the point." Zigway opens his desk and pulls out a file. He throws in on the desk. Lieutenant Post picks up the file. The look on his face tell a lot. Green snatched the file out of lieutenant Post hands. He was shocked at the name of the file. It was Mia Pond. Detective Ponds daughter who died at the YMCA six years ago. "How did you get this?" Detective Green ask. "Y'all police tend to forget the fire department has to do a report. So does the ambulance. Also Bridgeport hospital at the time had a two person file system. One on computer and one on a hard copy." Zigway explained with a smile on his face.

"How did you know about our case?" Lieutenant Post asked. "This is Bridgeport nothing is secret. If I know then you know everyone else knows." After Zigway said that lieutenant Post immediately gets up and start making phone calls. That gets Green thinking about the attempt on his life. "I know what you are thinking about." Zigway said like he is reading detective Green's mind. "I don't think it was your brother. Who sent those men to try to kill you." "Then who do you think did?" Green said while still cringing in pain. "I don't know? You know your brother has enemies. Plus this is looking like your brothers past is coming back to haunt him." Green begins to agree with Zigway.

Lieutenant Post gets off the phone. "I just got off the phone with agent Morales. She is moving all files to the F.B.I field office at downtown Bridgeport." Post just said. He then sits down and begins to read the medical file. Pacifically the autopsy. Lieutenant Post look changes so dramatically Green begins to tap him on the shoulder. Wondering what's wrong. "They held her under water. According to the autopsy report. She had hand prints on her shoulder." Lieutenant Post says. Detective Green stands up and begins pacing back and forth. Zigway seen Green do this before. He only does this when he is angry.

Green stopped pacing then he begins to say. "My brother covered up a murder. Then use this as leverage so he can gain power."Lieutenant Post agreed with what detective Green said. "Knowing it and proving it are two different things." Lieutenant Post said. "We need to get the Judge, the representative, and former district attorney Willcots to flip." "I agree lieutenant. Our best chance is the attorney. We may be able to flip him. Plus I need to talk to that nun again." Green said while looking at lieutenant Post. "Y'all is forgetting one thing." Both Lieutenant Post and detective Green look at Zigway with a confused look they don't know what he is talking about. Zigway begins to laugh then he says. "Oh my god. This is supposed to be Bridgeport finest?" Both Green and post feel insulted. It is showing on their face and body. "The race to find detective Pond. If Joe finds him you wont be able to flip nobody. If Joe's enemies find him the streets of Bridgeport will be fill with blood." Both Lieutenant Post and detective Green nod in agreement. With what Zigway said. "Another reason why I am transferring to Baltimore." Post looks shocked but detective Green didn't.

"So it was Joe's enemies that tried to kill me?" Green asked. Zigway gave that I don know shrug. They both stand up to exit. Lieutenant Post grabs the file and Green and him exit. They take the elevator down to the first floor we're they are met by captain Martinez and detective Hagan. Plus other plain clothes police officers. "What is going on captain?" Lieutenant Post said in a commanding tone. "We found Ashley's body. It looks like she was beaten to death. There was a lead pipe found next to the body." Detective Hagen said coldly. "We need to know your we're about since you left the crime scene on Gilman St?"

"He has been with me." Green and Post turn around and see Zigway. "You can also ask the mayor. He seen them come in my office." The plain clothes officers got into their car and left. Leaving captain Martinez and detective Hagen alone. "We're is her body?" Green ask. "This is Hagen's investigation stay out of this." Martinez says he then gets back into his car with Hagen driving. "They came here to arrest you. Hagen and Martinez is looking to find something on you. After this case leave the police department." After Zigway said that lieutenant Post immediately got into Zigway face then said. "Detective Green is a good police detective we need him." "Need him look at all the things y'all put him through. If he stays two things will happen. He will either get killed by a crooked police officer or one of Joe's enemies. Our Martinez and Hagen will frame him for sometime he didn't do."

Lieutenant Post paused for awhile thinking on what Zigway had said. He knows the fire chief is telling the truth. Post begins to put his head down. Know he has nothing to say. Plus he agrees with him. "We will talk about this after the case." Green said while putting his right hand on Zigway shoulder. "I will check on your daughter at the hospital." "Be carful Joe's wife is there." He nods then leave. Post and green gets in the car. They sit for five minutes then lieutenant Post says. "You have been through a lot the past few years. Plus this department has not showed their gratitude. Don't give up on the citizens please. They deserve justice." Post finishes then starts the car.

Chapter 33

Lieutenant Post and detective Green begins heading to the Catholic Church on east Main Street. Post who is driving the black police Sudan. Takes a glance at Green who is in the passenger seat. Who has a blank look on his face. Post is wondering if Green is okay. After hearing that his babies mother was found dead. "I am okay lieutenant." Green said coldly while still looking straight ahead. "It's understandable that you have feelings for her. Even though she tried to kill you." Green turns his head to Post then said. "I rather not talk about it. I slipped up and I got weak. I should have known she was spying on me. I will never make that same mistake again."

Green turns his head back away after he finishes. Lieutenant Post pulls the car over at Washington park. On Noble Avenue which is near east Main Street. He turns the car off looks at detective Green then said. "There was no way you would have known. What happened to you happened to plenty of people in the past." While lieutenant Post is talking Green continues to breathe hard. Like a person who is getting angry and more angry. Before Post can continue Green yell's out. "I am not those people. I should have known. This shows how incompetent I am. Plus it shows my failure to lead. Captain Martinez will use this. To say its my fault all those witnesses in the past cases that got killed." After Green said that lieutenant Post.

Begins to think. Then he turns to detective Green and says. "Which will propel him to be the new chief of police." They continue till they reach the Catholic Church on east Main Street. They park in the parking lot in the back. Him and lieutenant Post noticed that none of the priests are in. Because the assigned parking spot is empty. Post help Green out of the car. They knock on the door waiting for someone to answer. They knock for another five minutes before lieutenant Post tries the door. It opened immediately like it was unlocked. Post immediately waves down a passing police cruiser. This part of east Main Street is a very active.

There are a lot of call in this area. Shooting, hit and runs just to name a few. Two uniformed officers exit the car. Post explain the situation to them. Then tells detective Green to stay here. Lieutenant Post and the uniformed officers enter the building. Which is a house behind the church. Both the nuns and the priest live here. Sometimes they house kids who have nowhere to go. All three enter to building with their guns drawn. They begin checking the rooms on the first floor. Calling out hello very loudly. They all split up to cover more ground. After two minutes of searching someone yell's out lieutenant up stairs second floor. Post rushed to the second floor to one of the bedrooms in the back. To find the nun hanging from the ceiling. One of the officers immediately called it in.

Post orders the officers to creat a perimeter. Post then goes outside to let Green know what happened. Green slams his hand on the hood of the. Within five minutes the place was surrounded with police officers. Plus news reporters and people. The chief of police arrived on the scene. He is escorted to we're lieutenant Post and Green is. He is in is class a uniform. "What happened?" "We found the nun dead. She apparently hung her self." Lieutenant Post said. "Then get rid of all these police officers. Plus the crime scene unit. We are wasting money. Plus it's obvious she committed suicide." "I don't believe that's true chief." Green said. "You shouldn't be here detective. One you are nursing a gunshot wound and two you are under investigation."

After the chief said that. Detective Green charged the police chief. Grabbing him by the shirt screaming. "What the hell for?" "Your baby mother had access to information that got a number of witness killed. Spanning multiple cases." The chief said. Multiple police officers broke up the two. "As of right now you are under administrative leave." The chief then walks away. Detective Green takes his sling off. Lieutenant Post tries to stop him but fails. "I am going to finish this case. I don't give a fuck what he says."Green says while blood is trickles from his gunshot wound. "I will have one of my detective in my unit to investigate the nun." Post said. "We need to go to the federal building." Green said. While getting in the driver seat.

CHAPTER 34

Lieutenant Post and detective Green made it to the federal building. With Green having to. Change his shirt because of the blood from the bullet wound. Green begins to think maybe his stepfather had the right idea. While staring at the trunk of the car. Post sensing something is wrong. Walks to him and says. "What's wrong? You know I am going to help you get through this." Green looks at Post. "After this case I just might." Before he can finish Post stops him then says. "You are not quitting. I won't let you. Don't let you and your brothers enemies win." Before Post can finish he is interrupted. "Hello guys. We have a problem."

They look to see who it is and it's agent Morales. In her black suit looking sexy. Green start to see why his former partner married her. "Lieutenant Post you are allowed up and on this case. But you detective Green are not. It's because you have been suspended from the Bridgeport police department. And you have a competency Hearing Coming up." Both Lieutenant Post and detective Green were taken back at what she said. Post and Green new about the suspension but not about the hearing. By the looks on their face agent Morales she revealed something they didn't know.

They remain silent for five minutes then agent Morales says. "No one told you about the hearing?" "No they didn't. When is the hearing?" Green ask with lieutenant Post trying to calm him down. "Don't get mad at me. I thought you new. Did they tell you they found your nephew dead? His head was found in front of the police department." Detective Green started screaming out while tears came down his eyes. He was so loud people started rushing out of the federal building. Agent Morales trying to wave them off. Then two serous looking men in black suits. One is a middle age white male. The other is a well built black male. They talk to agent Morales for about two minutes. Till she comes back to lieutenant Post and detective Green. "Come up stairs." By the way she said that. Both Green and Post can tell that she is trouble. They followed her to the top floor of the federal building.

They were led to a conference room we're in the center of the room was a huge round table. On the walls is picture of the current president of the United States, and the F.B.I director. With small plants we're probably fake. Both Green and Post sat down. Then agent Morales leaves the room. Then a lady in a nursing uniform comes into the room. She has a medical bag with her. Green pulls up his shirt so she can tend to his gunshot wound. Soon she finishes she then leaves the room. Leaving Green and Post alone. They sat alone in the room for an hour before someone comes in.

In walks in agent Morales and the two men from earlier. They sat down in the big conference room table. Agent Morales had the look like a person that was just scolded. "Agent Morales was not suppose to tell you detective." Lieutenant Post and detective Green start to get angry. At what the agent said. "Calm down hear us out." The other agent. "We want to stay out of this. One we are against this hearing. This is a political move by captain Martinez. He is trying to get on the good graces of the new mayor." Green is starting to calm down. Agreeing with the the agent. Green begins to be mad at himself for not seeing this coming.

"The new mayor is leading in the polls. It looks like he will win by a landslide. Martinez is using you as a scapegoat for all those witnesses getting killed in the last three years. Captain Martinez may very well be your next police chief." After the agent finishes Green gets up pacing back and forth with his head down. "They are going to sideline him with this hearing. Bring all this information out in the hearing. The same information agent Morales wasn't supposed to tell him. Confused him to make him look guilty at the hearing." Lieutenant Post screamed out. "Yes it's a political tactic used by federal authorities all the time."

Green now wondering if not quitting after the last hearing was a good idea. He stops pacing and stares at the American flag. "We are asking you to stay off this case. Lieutenant Post you can stay on." After hearing that. Green storms out of the conference room with people yelling his name. He gets on the elevator before anyone can stop it. His phone begins to ring. He then turns his phone off. He exit the elevator with district marshal preventing him from leaving. Even though he flashed his badge. The agents from the conference room plus lieutenant Post. Arrived to the front door. We're the district Marshals are.

They ordered the marshals to release him. They take their hands off him. Then return to their post. Then the alarm that was on went off. So did the automatic door locks on the doors. "We apologize for the marshals for detaining you. We just want assurances that you will not interfere with the case." Detective Green nods his head in agreement. Him and post leave the federal building. The two agents watch them leave. Then one of them make a phone call. To order other two agents who are outside to watch them. The then hangs up the phone. Then says. "You know he still going to investigate." "Yea I know. It will help us find out who in the Bridgeport police department is corrupt." They turn around and head back upstairs.

CHAPTER 35

Lieutenant Post and detective Green enter the car. Post begins to drive when a text came through to his cell phone. He waited till he reached a red light to answer the text. One of the detective in his unit text him the address of detective Pond's wife. Lieutenant Post was shocked at the address the detective sent to him. He was so shocked other cars behind started to honked their horns because the light turned green. Post continues to drive. "Is everything ok?" Green asked feeling concerned. "What was in the text you received?" Post pulls in front of the Bridgeport library.

He explains what the text is. Then he tell him the address 76 A Karen court. Just like Post Green is shocked at the address. "She lives in the same condominium as Ms Willcots." Detective Green says. "We need to go talk to her. She may know we're her husband is." Lieutenant Post agrees with what detective Green said. "We are heading there now." Lieutenant Post said. He started the car back up heading towards Ms Pond address. Post took the highway to get to the address. It took them less than four minutes to reach the address.

They reach the address at Karen court. It is at the very end of the street. "We need to find out how long she has been living here." Detective Green said. Lieutenant Post sends a text message to one of his detective in his unit. They park near the forest at the end of the street. They exit the vehicle and head towards the address. All the condos look the same. The only thing that is different about them is that. Some of them has a A or a B. They reach the door. It's plain looking with a welcome sign on the door.

They can hear the tv on. It sounds like the news or soap operas. Lieutenant Post knocks on the door. They hear a person immediately working on the locks on the door. A middle aged white female. Opens the door. Lieutenant Post recognize her almost immediately. He remember seeing her in the benefits office of the Bridgeport police department. "I know why you are here. If he is doing the killings that they say. I don't blame him and will not help you." Ms Pond said coldly. "We need to find him. Your husband is the prime suspect. We understand why he is doing this." Lieutenant Post said. "No you don't. Your partner lieutenant. His brother helped those girls get away with murder." Ms Pond screams out.

Out of nowhere they hear someone yell. "Freeze Police put your hands in the air now." Both Post detective Green and Ms Pond run towards the parking lot. We're they see both the F.B.I and the Bridgeport police officers which one of the detective from Posts unit. Surround a blue Chevy Nova with two black males in it. Lieutenant Post runs to support the officers and F.B.I agents. While detective Green stay to keep Ms Pond safe. The two black males exit the vehicle very slowly. The uniformed officers put handcuffs on them. While lieutenant Post and the agents approach the detective from Post unit. One of the federal agents approach Green and say. "We will take over interrogation of this witness. You have been compromised even more detective. You will be briefed later."

They took Ms Pond to a arriving suv and they left. Detective Green approach lieutenant Post and his detective. Who Green recognize as John Hannan. "Hello rock. What is going on?" Green said with a smile on his face. "Please stop calling me that." John said. John continue to talk to lieutenant Post. "The nun was killed and made to look like she committed suicide." Post has a smile on his face. So does detective Green. "The guys in the car we just arrested. Bought this rope at a local Home Depot. The I noticed I recognize them. So I checked every photo and every crime scene photo. It appears they have been following you detective Green. For how long I don't know."

Detective Green was shocked at what he just heard. Plus he was angry for not knowing and picking up the tale. "Captain Martinez is going to use this to blame you for all the witness killed. In past investigation plus other problems." Lieutenant Post says. "Also the feds has the judge brought to the interrogation room." John says. They both climbed into the car and head to the police department. Once they arrived at the police department. They walked in to see a lot of federal agents. They continue to interrogation room one where they see the judge and his lawyer being interrogated by agents Morales and captain Martinez. Detective Green feels a tap on his shoulder. It's the police chief. He motions detective Green to follow him. He and lieutenant Post follow the police chief. The enter captain Martinez office which is right down the hall. Captain Martinez is already their sitting at his desk. So detective Green enters then office along with lieutenant Post.

"The lieutenant doesn't have to be here chief." Captain Martinez says. The police chief raised his hand as is to silence Martinez. Green sits down in front of Martinez desk. "No need to stand detective. You won't be here long." Martinez says without a word from the police chief. The chief approach detective Green then says. "We will have a hearing in a couple of weeks. To determine your incompetence. As a police detective in the city of Bridgeport. A number of things have popped. That question your incompetence. You are allowed to have your union delegate at the hearing. Your lawyer already made a motion to appear to represent you." Detective Green is getting angry at what is being told him.

He knows all this is captain Martinez doing. "Until then detective you are put on administrative leave with pay. I need your gun." The chief hold out his hand waiting for detective Green to hand over his gun. Green reluctantly do so. "Your back up also detective." Martinez says with a wicked grin on his face. Green hands over his back up gun. Then walks out of Martinez office. Trying to keep his cool. Lieutenant Post follow him then drag him to the empty situation room. We're lieutenant post motion him to sit down.

"You are going to get through this. Captain Martinez is just using you so he can be chief." Post says while Green has a cold look on his face. "I don't know how your brothers lawyer knows. But I recommend you use him. He is perfect for this situation. Detective Green give him a look like he didn't believe he just said that. Then a knock came at the door. Then in walks agent Morales. She is looking like a person who just lost a soccer game. "I have some bad news and you might not like it. Because of your excellent investigation detective Green. We have enough evidence to show that the judge helped cover up a murder."

A smile came over Green face. "The judge then says. He will testify against your brother detective Green. And everyone involved. In detective Turner's daughter death. But under one condition. He wants complete immunity from prosecution." Detective Green slams his hand against a chair next to him in protest. "If not he will say during the twenty years on the bench he fixed a lot of cases." Both lieutenant Post and detective Green were taken back at what was said. Because they know if the judge say that. A whole lot of prisoners will be released. Both detective Green and lieutenant Post know the F.B.I has to make the deal. "We have no choice but to make the deal. The federal prosecutor is drawing up the paperwork." Agent Morales finishes.

"Any news on the whereabouts of detective Turner?" Lieutenant Post asked. "We can't find him. Since he wasn't at his ex house. We don't know we're to look." "I will continue searching for him I might have some idea we're he is at." Detective Green says. "You are on suspension pending a hearing." Lieutenant Post says. " I don't care someone has to stop him and bring him in alive." Both Morales and Post agrees with what Green said. Agent Morales leaves the room leaving both lieutenant Post and detective Green alone. "We need to talk to Turner's old partner. Maybe he might know we're he is hiding." Green suggested. Lieutenant Post agrees and they both walk to a room on the first floor of the police department.

It's marked personnel files authorized officers only. Post pulls out a key card and the automatic door locks. Became unlocked. They walked into a huge room filled with file cabinets. A plane looking room. They noticed a computer at the far end of the room. They walked to the computer. Post used his key card to sign in. He is immediately in the system. He put in detective Turner's full name and rank. His picture popped up immediately. Post scrolls till he finds who was Turner's partner. His partner was detective Gabriel Mosby. "I know him he was a good detective. He had a 90% conviction rating. It says he he retired when Turner retired. He is currently working as a private detective.

His office is in Stamford." Post says while writing down the address. Post logs himself out of the system and they both leave. They walk to the car which is parked in the back of the police station. They are met by the chief of police. Both Post and Green are taken back by seeing him. "I know where you two are going. I am going with. And for the record I am against the hearing detective. Captain Martinez is just using you." He climbs in the front seat with Green in the back and lieutenant Post driving.

CHAPTER 36

They reach the the office building in Stamford. The chief was taken back when he saw the name on the building. The Dickerson building. Both the chief and lieutenant Post turn to look at detective Green. Who has the same look as them. Green then noticed they were looking at him then says. "I didn't know he owns the building." Both the chief and the lieutenant nod in agreement. "You what this means. The private investigator works for my brother." Detective Green says. As they walk to the main entrance to the building. They see two Stamford police officers at the outside tables drinking coffee. At the small restaurant that is located on the first floor of the building.

The two police officers recognize the Bridgeport police chief immediately. They both motioned themselves toward Green, lieutenant Post and the police chief. While one of the officers was radioing dispatch. "Did you notify dispatch?" Post asked. "Yes the watch commander wants to know what are you doing?" One of the officers replied. "We are here to question private investigator Gabriel Mosby." Lieutenant Post replied. After they said that both officers had a strange look on their face. Like the look your parents get when they say to themselves. What did he do this time. "You recognize the name officers?" Post asked. "Yes he is currently under investigation with homicide unit. We have to notify them."

The officers radio for the Homicide unit of the Stamford police department. Their captain said he was on his way with two of his detective. They sat outside for ten minutes. Then a dark blue Sedan pulls up. With three men exiting the vehicle. All three were wearing expensive black suit. Like if they were working at walls street. If it wasn't for their police bages you wouldn't think they were cops. The older one must be the captain. The chief new him immediately. They immediately shook hands and talk. "Hello lieutenant Post and detective Green. I am captain Bill McLaren." Said the older gentleman. "These two with me is detective Abner Finn, and Edwin Cheney."they all shook hands then they begin to explain why they are here. "We have been investigating the private investigator. For a couple of unsolved murders that were witness in our cases." One of the detective said. "He had a talent for finding people. His father was and excellent tracker for the US marshal" "that wasn't in his file we have in Bridgeport."Lieutenant Post said

"On his birth certificate it must only show his mother. When you see that when he applied to be a police officer that is what log in. He must have found his father using police resources. It obvious he kept it to him self." The captain said. They entered the building were they are met by a lady at the desk. Who is surrounded by five security guards. "How may we help you?" "We are here to see private investigator Mosby." "He is on the tenth floor and as for you Michael Green. Do you want me to let your brother know you are here? The meeting starts in two hours." "No please don't and next time don't call me by my first name."detective Green said.

They leave the front desk and head to the tenth floor. Took the elevator up with lieutenant Post looking at the security camera in the elevator giving it his middle finger. Smiling while doing it. They reach the office door for Mosby. Where they see another set of elevators. Except these elevators are guarding by security. "We're do those elevators go?" Lieutenant Post asked. Those go to my brothers office his inner sanctum. They make their way to Mosby office we're they find it slightly open.

All of them pulled out their guns. Post orders the uniformed officers to remain at the door. They walk in and see file papers everywhere on the floor. File cabinets on the floor. The office is a complete mess. They found Mosby dead with three gunshot wounds to the chest. Center mass. Captain McLaren call in crime scene tech and additional officers. With ten minutes the building was locked down. Crime scene techs everywhere. Uniformed officers begin questioning the security officers who were guarding the elevator entrance to mr Dickerson.

Ten minutes after the crime scene tech came then came the F.B.I.

Who was fuming mad that the chief of police in Bridgeport didn't inform them of their lead. They were immediately updated by Stamford police then told there office is under investigation. They were all interrupted by one of the crime scene techs. An average white male with glasses. "We went through some of the files that was scattered on the floor. They were files on everyone involved in the YMCA drowning case. Along with the remaining people that are alive and in witness protection. With address." After he said that the F.B.I immediately got on the phone and made some calls. While on of their agents were being told they will be visited by people from Washington.

One of the Stamford police officers approached lieutenant Post and detective Green. "We talked to the security guard at the elevator. They say there was a delivery once a month. By a company that delivers water for the water cooler." "There's no water cooler in the office." Bridgeport Police chief says. "Same thing I said. Turner use that as his cover to sneak in and out." Says the officer. "What was the name of the company?" Detective Green asked. "WB Mason. We already are asking them for their employees records and everything."

The officer turns away and leaves. The federal agents got off their phones after being on them for twenty minutes. One of the federal agents says. "All witnesses are dead with their throats slashed and a rat in their mouths. Except for one. The representative the guy that works in Hartford. He hung himself. He recorded a video confession. We are uploading the video now. He also sent the confession to every news outlet." "Joe Dickerson got to them. We can't prove it because he just use us as a alibi. Since we locked down the whole building." Lieutenant Post says. "I guess the private investigator was playing both sides." Says the Stamford police detective.

One of the CSI technicians came to them and put a finger over his mouth. As to single to keep quiet. He then pointed to the central air grate. They can see a microphone. Detective Green wrote on a piece of paper. "This whole room is tapped. My brother must've tapped his office. Green then ripped up the paper. They all exited to office and closed the door. "Get a warrant for those tapes now." Says Bridgeport Police chief. "The Stamford police captain ordered his two detectives to go upstairs and bring down Joe Dickerson. Joe came down two minutes later with his lawyer. "I heard everything on the news. My client has been here all day. You even locked down the building." Says Joe lawyer. He opened a briefcase and handed the police captain four cd's. "These are audio recordings of Mr Mosby office. We had is office tapped for two days." Stamford police captain took the cd's "anything else you need to get a warrant." Two seconds later a Stamford police officer came with a warrant. "Both the judge and the district attorney are downstairs in the restaurant having coffee. Says the uniformed officer. "Tell the CSI tech and every uniform officer to search this entire building. Then the captain focuses his attention on the lawyer. I need a copy of Joe's telephone records now." The lawyer opens his briefcase again and handed him a copy. Who then the captain handed it to lieutenant Post.

Chapter 37

Lieutenant Post and detective Green along with Bridgeport Police Chief Gill Ridges. Are at the Stamford police station. All of them are in a huge conference room with pictures of former Stamford police chief's. Federal agents are there also along with the state police. Who are on the phone. They been on the phone ever since they arrived thirty minutes ago. They finally got off the phone. The huge one white male with Sargent bars on his state police uniform. He reminded Green of Brian Urlacher. A famous Chicago bears football player. "Hello guys I am here to inform you that representative of Bridgeport is dead." There was a big gasp in the room.

That news took put everyone in shock. The Sargent continues by saying. "He committed suicide. He hung himself. Using a rope. But before he killed himself. He made a video confession. Which he sent to every media outlet in the country. He confessed to everything including helping the judge keep people out of jail and put people in. And names everyone who was on the take and working for Joe

Dickerson." They was a long pause. Before Lieutenant Post could say anything the Sargent continued. "We are typing arrest warrants right now. We are also detaining several Bridgeport Police officers on numerous charges. The state police will take control of your police department for the time being. As for you detective Green that hearing is still in place. We know you have nothing to do with what you're brother was doing. But several other things came to light that might cost you your job." After he finished he left the room and detective Green sat down putting his hands in his face.

After twenty minutes of silence the chief of police in Stamford. Who was on the phone the entire time says. "My sources telling me that. The only reason they are continuing with the hearings is to make you a scapegoat. Somebody has to be blamed for all the witnesses being killed in your city. Witnesses in high profile cases." Lieutenant Post spoke and said. "Let me guess it's captain Martinez?" The chief shook his head yea. "He is trying to be the next police chief of Bridgeport." Stamford police chief says.

Then In walks a woman in police uniform. Wearing glasses with blonde hair. "They located the missing WB Mason worker. He lives in a condo on white plains road in Trumbull. Just outside Bridgeport police jurisdiction. I notified Trumball Police and the state police they are already on their way." All but the Stamford police officers ran out of the conference room.

Chapter 38

When they arrive. Detective Green recognized the area. "We were just here. We interviewed the reporters wife." Lieutenant Post agrees with detective Green. The scene is full of Trumball police officers, Bridgeport police officers, and state police officers. They exited the vehicle and was immediately met by the state police. "Tell your police officer to leave the scene. They are out of their jurisdiction and under investigation." Says the state trooper. Captain Martinez tries to make his point heard. Bridgeport Police chief orders his officers to leave the scene. Captain Martinez complied with the order.

As soon as captain Martinez left a shot was fired. They all ran to the spot where the shot was fired. They find two Bridgeport swat officers standing over detective Turner's dead body. The WB Mason worker alive but covered in blood. Immediately then chief puts the swat officers on administrative leave. "We were ordered to breach." Said the officers who had the look of confusion on their faces. The officers leave while being escorted by state police. Lieutenant Post and detective Green stay to process the scene

They first check on the the hostage. He appears to be fine except covered in blood. The blood not being his. Post let him know they have questions for him later. Paramedics came and look over the hostage. Lieutenant Post joins detective Green along with CSI technician in processing the scene.

Green finds numerous papers on the wall. With drawing of all the people they have in protection. Along with the times for shift change. "Chief come and see this." Yells detective Green. The chief along with lieutenant Post and some state troopers. They were all in shock and amazed. His surveillance was so on point. They even found files he had on federal agents. "You might want to check your surveillance tapes at the federal building. He might of used the WB mason uniform to get in." Lieutenant Post says to the federal agents who immediately left the room on their phones.

The state troopers ordered the forensic team to take pictures and gather the evidence. While walking around detective Green noticed a door. That was near the master bedroom. Where the bathroom should be. Green tried the door but it was locked. He called to one of the forensic technicians to try to unlock the door. After five minutes the technician was able to open the door. The technician walks in and finds more photos but this time of Joe Dickerson.

His movements who he talks to everything. Both Green and the chief of police is happy. The let the state troopers take the evidence. Green walks outside relieved this is over. But is worried what is going to happen with his brother. With this new evidence a lot is going to come out about his family. Green begins to think maybe his stepfather was right on transferring out. Green feels a tap on his shoulder he turns around and finds its captain Martinez. "This new evidence doesn't let you off the hook. We are still having that hearing and I will have your badge detective." Martinez left and went back to his police cruiser and ordered his driver to o drive.

"Just to let you know detective. Captain Martinez is delaying his hearing until we finish with your brother. I guess he hopes we find something on you. That he can use." Green looks to his left and it's captain of troop G of the state police. "Do me a favor detective don't leave the state of Connecticut." State trooper said while walking away. Detective Green walks leaves the condo and walks outside. He is met by lieutenant Post who stops to talk to the detective and says. "Somebody put detective Turner on to this. Who ever it was new if they give him some information he would figure the rest out." Green nods in agreement. On what lieutenant Post said.

Then detective Green remembers something from earlier in the investigation. "Detective Turner worked at Sing Sing prison. In New York. Then one day disappeared. One of the prisoners are probably the one." Lieutenant Post agrees with Green's statement. "We need to contact agent Morales. I will to since I am not being watched" lieutenant Post says. They both climbed back into the car and head towards the police station while lieutenant Post is on the phone.

CHAPTER 39

They arrived at the Bridgeport Police Station. They entered the station through the back door. When they pulled up they see several state police cars. Along with international affairs cars too. Both detective Green and the chief of police is wondering what is going on. When they enter to police station they are met by the desk Sargent. Older white male who looks like he is about to retire any day now. "What is going on Sargent?" The chief asked. "Several of our police officers are being arrested for corruption. It's stemming from the representative video confession that went viral. plus they arrested the judge which caused all his cases into question. Every criminal in the state is filing for a appeal. Plus the state has a witness chief." "Who is the witness?" The chief asked.

The desk sergeant took his time to answer. Both Green and the chief can sense the fear on him. "It's Detective Green's and Joe Dickersons Father Paul Dickerson aka the Godfather." Detective Green was taken back at what he heard. He thought his father was dead. His brother told him he was dead. "You are lying." Green yelled out "He is dead. He was shot and killed in his home." Green continues to yell out. "There is a explanation for that detective. Let's use your office chief." Said the attorney general for Connecticut. They followed him to the chief's office. On the way Green can see several police officers put in handcuffs by men in suits. He also sees captain Martinez on a podium making a statement to the press. Green knows Martinez will use this to become the next chief of police. Before he gets on the elevator he can see in the distance. The main interrogation room he thinks he sees a ghost. The person he sees is his father who he thought is dead. Green begins to think that maybe the desk sergeant. Was telling the truth. They finally made it to the chief's office. We're they all sat down except the attorney general. "According to the federal Judge who was on the take and records kept my the representative that we found. Your father was kept in different prisons under assumed names."

Everyone is silent at what he said. "Then who the hell did Joe bury in his father's suppose grave?" Lieutenant Post asked. "We currently have a team digging up the body now. We couldn't wait for your permission detective Green." Green nods in approval. "Your father is giving us everything on your brother. We are picking him up now. Unfortunately the hearing on you is still on. That I can't stop. I tried but can't. Captain Martinez is heading it. You won't go to jail but you can lose your job. He is claiming incompetence of becoming of a police officer." Detective Green slams his hand on the chief's desk. They try to calm him down. Blood starts flowing from his gunshot wound.

After he calmed down detective Green pulls out his badge. He then slams it on the desk and says. "I quit. I am done with this department." Everyone is shocked at what he did. "We can fight this detective." Lieutenant Post says. Green continues to walk out of the office. He continued to his desk and begin cleaning it out. When he is stopped by a female officer. Who shows him he is bleeding. The female officer continues to clean and bandage the wound. When the chief comes to him. "Clean out your desk later. Go to the hospital and get that wound taken care of." Before the chief could leave Green stopped him. Then says. "My father was held at a prison under a false name right?"

The chief nods his head yes. "Then what if he was held at a prison that detective Turner worked at and new who he was." "I know we're your going with this Green." Says the attorney general. "We investigated and they were. At sing sing prison. There is nothing we can charge your father on. Even though we know he set this whole thing in motion. He is clean and beside he was held against his will.

Both New York and Connecticut want this to go away. Later former detective." The attorney general leaves and toward the room we're Green father is along with his lawyer. Lieutenant Post tapes Green on the shoulder and motions him to follow him. They walk till they reach the car in the back of the police station we're they see a black suv pull up. Then three federal agents exit along with Joe Dickerson in handcuffs. "I will be out in a hour bro watch." Joe says while smiling. As they lead him to the police station.

CHAPTER 40

As soon as former detective Green arrives at Bridgeport Hospital. Nurse immediately tends to his gun shot wounds. The nurse gave him lip about leaving the hospital and not letting the staff finish patching the wound. After the nurse finished putting stitches on. The doctor walks in and begins to say. "There is a woman here. Who claims to be your sister in law. She is asking to see your daughter" "Does she talk with a southern accent and looks like the mother from the tv show the parkers." Green asked. The doctor nods his head yes. "Take me to her. She is okay." Green fallows the doctor to the children ward. When they walked in the room Green smiles as he sees his former sister in law.

His brother divorced her and married a younger Hispanic woman. Who's brother is the head of the Latin kings. She is holding the baby and feeding the baby. She has a smile on her face when she sees him. "Hello Susan." Says Green while he kisses her on the cheek. Green looks back at the doctor then says. "She is okay to visit. When can I take my daughter home?" "Tomorrow you can but you still have to fill out the birth certificate and name the child." "I will get back to you on that." Green finished. Susan gives Green a look. A look Green knows well. "I have been busy. That's what taking so long." Green says.

"I know that is what I am here to talk to you about. I know you are quitting the police force." Green is taken back at what she said. Green doesn't know how she knows when he just made that decision a couple of hours ago. "By the look on your face you are wondering how I know. You forget Bridgeport Police Department is corrupt as hell. Everyone on the streets knows." Before Green could say anything there was a huge commotion in the hallway. Green signals Susan to stay in the hospital room. While he investigates the commotion. As soon as he gets in the hallway he sees. A bunch of reporters yelling questions at Green's father. Who looks like he is enjoying the spotlight. He is big and strong sporting a white suit with hat. He reminds him of those old Italian mobsters. The hospital security is trying to push the reporters back. Green walks back into the room followed by his father.

He is shocked when he sees Susan. "What would bring your fat country ass to Bridgeport? Atlanta to much for you?" Green father says then he starts laughing loudly. "I came here to support Green" Susan pointing at Green while talking. "I heard he got shot and I flew over here. Someone got to make sure he is okay." Paul starts to get angry. Green can see it. Before anyone can say anything the doctor walks in. He hands Green some papers to sign then says. "Instead of tomorrow you can take your daughter home." The doctor left immediately. Then Susan says. "I will be downstairs with the baby. I will wait for you."

Green acknowledged what she says. She leaves taking the baby with her. Now Paul and Green were the only two left in the room. "Now that we are alone we can have that conversation." Paul said with a wicked smile on his face. "It's good that you left the police department. You see me and your brother are different as night and day. I would've killed your ass for betraying your people's." After Paul said that Green got closer to him. So close he can feel his breath. "I don't blame you for hooking up with your brothers ex. She has a nice ass." Green immediately grabs his father slamming him to the door. Shattering the window.

Which draws the attention of all the security guards on the unit. They separated them. While Paul begins to laugh. "It seems I struck a nerve boy. Remember what I said. Stay a civilian. I'm about to show you some real gangster shit." Paul walks away laughing. He is joined by several men. Green recognizes them from the east end of Bridgeport. Mainly from fifth street. Also known as bloody fifth. Green waits awhile then leaves. When he makes it to the front of Bridgeport Hospital. He sees his former sister-in-law. She is still holding his daughter. As he walks to the truck she rented. A blue Ford expedition. She begins to o say. "I saw the people you're father left with. I guess the rumors I heard is true. Your brother lost the East end. It's about to get real bloody in Bridgeport. Get in the car we will talk more at your house." They get into the truck and leave.

CHAPTER 41

They reach Green's house. They notice several Bridgeport police vehicles in front of the house. Green looks at Susan. Who also glances at him. Both thinking the same thing. When they pulled up to the house. They are approached by a uniformed police officer. Who is followed by a man Green recognize. It's Lieutenant Post. "Hello Green. Your security alarm went off. I have uniform officers securing the house now." Then out of nowhere Lieutenant Post gets a call over the radio. He then turns around and starts running.

Green jumps out of the truck and runs in the same direction as Lieutenant Post. They ran to the door when uniformed officers are coming out with a male in handcuffs. The suspect is a Hispanic man who is covered with tattoos that reads MS 13. Lieutenant Post orders other uniformed officers to do a complete search of the home. He also ordered crime scene technicians to the house. Post approach Green then says. "I think you should find somewhere else to sleep tonight." "I will sleep in a hotel tonight." Green says with a hotel already in mind. "Not the Trumbull Marriott." Says the federal agent who arrived on the scene.

"Agent Morales. Why not the Marriott?" Green asked. "You're brother owns that particular one through one of his subsidiaries company." Agent Morales said. Green and lieutenant Post were shocked. They looked at each other with the look of shock on their faces. "I have to give to your brother he is smart. It must of took you all week to figure that out." Susan says while smiling. Agent Morales walks toward Susan with her heels clicking. "No it didn't Susan. Aren't you under investigation by the Atlanta Police Department. You are the head of one of the biggest gangs In Atlanta." Morals says in front of Susan face. They stare at each other like they are about to fight. "How about the holiday inn downtown? It's empty." Lieutenant Post says. Everyone nods in agreement.

Then Bridgeport Police officers escort the suspect out of the house. Then they put in in the back of the squad car. Green then turns to Susan then begins saying in a angry tone. "We need to have a conversation later." She nods then gets back into the truck. Two police officers stay with the truck while Green enters the house to grab a couple of things. They are escorted to the empty holiday inn hotel. Located downtown Bridgeport. They are met by a police officer in swat uniform. The officer gives them the all clear. Green with his daughter is on one floor. While Susan is staying on another floor.

Susan walks into her room. She can tell it's the president suite. She closed the door. Then turns around to find a Beretta pointed to her face. She realized it's Green's brother Joe Dickerson. "I had nothing to do with that. I swear to you Joe. I will never harm Green nor his daughter." Susan says while trying to act hard. But she is really scared. "I hope so. Nobody harms my family. Especially my niece. Who was just born. Don't worry I have the person who sent him. I will get the information I need. If i find out you have something to do with this.

You and your entire crew in Atlanta. Will die. If you are wondering how I got in. I own this city. Good by Susan." Joe then walks into the bathroom, and he was gone. Susan walks to the bathroom door open it up. Just to find nobody there. Her heart starts pounding. It's been a long time since she was this scared. She knows Joe was powerful but not like this. She hears a knock on her door. She goes into her suite case and grabs a gun. She cocks it back to make sure it's loaded. She hears a voice on the tenth knock. She recognize the voice. She holstered the gun then open the door.

She lets Green into her room. He is holding the baby. Green sets the baby down on the bed. Then walks to her and says. "What is wrong did something scare you?" Susan begins to tell Green about her encounter with Joe. After hearing her Green. Then walks into the bathroom. Knocking on the walls while in the bathroom. He then finds a hidden pathway behind the sink. Green closes the pathway with a smile on his face. "What is so funny?" Susan asks. "My brother loves history. Especially Chicago history. There was a guy by the name of H H Holmes. He owned a hotel that had a lot of secret rooms and hidden pathways. Which he used to kill his victims. I guess my brother did the same thing except he used the hidden pathways to collect information." After he said that Susan was even more scared of Joe.

Green asked Susan to watch the baby while he goes to clean out his desk at the police station.

CHAPTER 42

Green pulls up to the police station. He walks into the front entrance. He sees a young officer at the Sargent desk. The young officer buzzes Green into the police station. Green walks in and it's a ghost town. It's usually somewhat busy at seven pm. But it's quite very quiet. Green sees lieutenant Post at the coffee table. He walks to lieutenant Post then says. "Where is everyone?" "Post takes a sip of his coffee then says. "Everyone is at Murphy's Law for Sargent Clark retirement party." Green slaps himself in the head like a person who has forgotten something.

Then the lieutenant replied. "I'm going down there once I finish my report." Green figured he would especially with all his things that has been happening. Green pulls out a box and's starts cleaning out his desk. With in ten minutes a knock on his desk stops him. Captain Martinez along with detective Hagen. Stops Green from what he is doing. Lieutenant Post seeing everything from his office joins him. "So you are his lawyer now lieutenant?" Captain Martinez says. "No I am captain. And you know I represent both Green and his brother. What do you want with my client?" My brothers lawyer says.

"We need to ask him questions concerning his motion detection system in his house. It looks like are suspect had the code to disarm the alarm." They were all shocked by what was said. Green immediately looks toward the interrogation room. We're his brother is at. Knowing what he's thinking captain Martinez says. "We're thinking the same thing." Martinez smiling afterwards.

"No, my brother didn't know the password. But my dead baby's mother did." Everyone has a shocking look on their face. Then captain Martinez says. "This still doesn't rule out your brother. He could have hired her to spy on you." "Unless you have anything to charge my client this interrogation is over." Green's lawyer says. "We were just having a conversation." Martinez says. Captain Martinez leaves so does the lawyer. Leaving lieutenant Post and Green alone. Green lawyer returned to his brother in the interrogation room. Where they are probably talking about what just happened. He can see his brother turned to take a glance at Green.

Green continues to empty his desk putting his belongings into a box. Lieutenant Post returns to his office. While Green continues to put his stuff into the box. He takes a moment to look at some of the rewards he won. Over the years. He begins to remember how much he loved the job. How much he loved being a police officer. Now he doesn't. He figures maybe he would go to Baltimore and work as a fire inspector. Since his stepfather is going down there to run the fire department. As he puts the last thing in the box he is approached by the chief of police.

"Is there any way I can talk you out of this.?" Green shakes his head no. Which leaves the chief disappointed. Before he can say anything else the rest of the police officers in the department. Is seen running outside very fast. Both Green and the chief are wondering what is going on. The phone at Greens desk begins to ring. The chief answers the phone. He slams it on the receiver. Then motions Green to follow him. They run to a waiting police car. Then immediately arrive at the scene of the crime.

They are about seven ambulances and a sea of police officers. Green recognizes the smoke in the air as automatic gunfire. Paramedics are pulling bodies out of a local bar. The same bar Green's fellow police officer was having a retirement party for the desk Sargent.

Green follows the police chief to the crime scene tape. We're he is stopped by captain Martinez. "He is a citizen now." Martinez says with a smile on his face. They are approached by detective Hagen. Who points to two uniformed officers. Then says. "I want you to detain former detective Michael Green." Before police could detain Green. Martinez and the chief say. "Green has nothing to do with this. He was at the police department cleaning out his desk. Plus, someone was waiting to kill him at his house." Hagen orders the police to stand down. Then he orders them to pick up Green's father and brother. Captain Martinez says again. "His brother is also at the police department speaking to the district attorney." Then detective Hagen says. So y'all are using the Al Capone defense." Hagen walks away. Green begins to walk back to the police department to finish cleaning up his desk.

Chapter 43

As Green takes that long walk up the stairs. Also called the courthouse steps. Because at the top of the steps is the golden hill courthouse. He begins to think. Is it a good idea to leave the police department. Was he making the right decision. He feels sad for all those police officers who are killed and maybe injured. He would have loved to be on this case. Then Green says to himself that he has a daughter to think about. As he walks past city hall, he can hear more ambulance. He walks to the front door of the police department.

The desk Sargent buzzes him in. As he takes the elevator to the second floor. He sees two men in suits at his desk. They are going through his boxes. Green also noticed. Lieutenant Post at the desk arguing with the men. Green runs to join lieutenant Post. Once he gets their Green says. "What is going on? Why are you going through my things?" "We are internal affairs. Twenty police officers were shot seven are confirmed to be dead. Thirteen injured." The other guy in a suit comes in and says. "Two more just died at Bridgeport Hospital."

A flood of emotions just came through Green. One of the detectives from internal affairs takes a phone call. Then says. "They found the suspects five of them. They are all dead from automatic gunfire. The guns found on the scene match the same caliber of bullets found at the police massacre. The chief is putting a rush on ballistic testing to confirm." Then lieutenant Post says. "We're was the suspect found?" "The Remington arms factory near Seaside Park" says the detective from internal affairs. Then the other says to Green. "Don't leave Bridgeport." They walk away and leave the department. Leaving lieutenant Post and Green alone. Green begins cursing out loud. With lieutenant Post trying to calm him down. The desk Sargent comes to lieutenant Post and speaks. "You have a call lieutenant. At the front desk. If you want, I can transfer it to your office." Lieutenant Post nods his head yes and heads for his office.

Post remains in his office for about one hour. Then comes out with a smile on his face. "You are in the clear. The suspect that was caught in your house that was going to kill you. Is part of the same gang that did the massacre." Green has a look of shock on his face. Then in walks Green's father. Accompanied by two police officers, and his lawyer. Green is fueled with anger seeing his father. Lieutenant Post knowing his thoughts says. "We don't know if it was him. Finished packing and go I will keep you updated." Lieutenant Post leaves and follows them to the interrogation room.

Green finishes packing then begins bringing the boxes to his car. The desk Sargent helping him. As the last box is loaded, he feels someone behind him. He immediately turns around with his gun in his hand. And it's his father. "If I wanted to kill I would son. Smart thing leaving the police department. Seeing that it's open season on cops." Greens father says with a smile on his face. After he says that Green pulls out a loaded 45 and puts it to his father's temple. "You better pull that trigger motherfucker. Or those guys behind you will kill you." Out of nowhere three men pulled out with their weapons out.

Then they are surrounded by a sea of police officers. Led by Lieutenant Post. "Ahh saved by the bitches. In blue." Green's father said. They all put their guns down and surrendered to the police. All were put in handcuffs except Greens father. Green is then led to lieutenant Post office were the handcuffs were removed. Post leaves and brief captain Martinez on what happened. After about twenty minutes Lieutenant Post returned. He sat down then said. "Captain Martinez wants to charge you with possession of a deadly weapon. I was able to convince him not to. You are free to go. As for your fathers crew they are being charged plus we have to tapes from the video camera outside." Green got up and shakes Lieutenant Post hands and leaves. He made it to the building he is staying at downtown Bridgeport. Which is the former holiday inns hotel. His former sister in law is cleaning the baby. "I made my decision I am moving. I'm leaving with my stepfather. Watch my daughter while I make the arrangements." She nods in agreement then Green leaves again.

Chapter 44

Green made it to his house near Beardsley Park. The crime scene tape is still visible. Green begins to wonder were are the police officers. Usually there are police officers at the crime scene. Till told other wise. Green pulls up to the driveway. This time he remembers his gun. He takes out his backup gun. Which is under the driver's seat. He approached the house quietly. Trying to avoid the window. He knows who ever is here most likely seen him already. He tries the door which is unlocked. He opens it. He hears noises in in the kitchen. Before he can make a move a voice screams out. "Put that gun away and get some of this pizza. It's from Captain's your favorite." Green recognized the voice. As his brother Joe Dickerson.

He walks into the kitchen seeing his brother eating a large pepperoni pizza. He can smell the pepperoni pizza as he enters the kitchen. Green just stands in the doorway. "I heard what happened with our father. Outside of the police department." Green is taken back by how fast he found out. "You actually pulled out a gun on our father. You must've had a reason. The real reason I am here is to try to convince you to stay in Bridgeport. Don't go to Baltimore with that guy that claims to be our stepfather. Just because he married our mother a week before she died. Don't make him family."

Green is again shocked by how come his brother knows what he is leaving. "I'm leaving bro I don't want to raise my daughter in this corrupt city." Joe rises from the kitchen table and is face to face with his brother. "First you betray your family and become a police officer. You arrest everyone that looked out for you and call you family."

Green can sense the anger in his voice. As he speaks. "I told you years ago when you visited me in prison. You are alive because of me. You know what we do to rats do you. You know the rules to the game. You took a oath not to betray your family." At that moment Joe pulled out a gun and pointed at Green. "Don't worry about your daughter I will raise her." Then out of nowhere several shots rang out. Both Joe and Green ducked for cover. The shooters continued shooting for five minutes. After the shooting stopped. Green pulls his gun out. His brother magically disappears. He runs outside with his weapon drawn. Not a car in sight. Two minutes later police officers arrived. Green had his hands raised with his gun on the ground.

The officers secured Green and his gun until Lieutenant Post arrived. With captain Martinez. Post released Green. Then Green explained what happened. He even provided video evidence from his ring camera. They begin to process the scene. There are about fourteen crime scene tech processing the house. One of the crime scene techs came to Green and Post then say. "It looks like the shooting was concentrated on the person on your front left." After the tech said that. Lieutenant Post immediately got on the radio asking for police officers to search for Joe Dickerson. Green went upstairs to gather his belongings. The techs are still processing the things after a hour of him packing.

After Green loads the last bag Lieutenant Post came toward him to try to plead his case on why Green should stay. After Green repeatedly said no. One of the uniformed officers came to them then said. "We found blood on the back porch. Then there is a trail of blood that leads to the street about a mile up." Green follows Lieutenant Post and Green follows the police officer. They follow the blood trail to a house right behind Green. The back door is open. Seeing this Lieutenant Post calls for backup and orders Green to stay put.

Backup arrives in about two minutes. They breach the house from the front and back. Some of the crime scenes tech from Green house. Walked over to this one. The Lieutenant waved Green to come in. He walks into the house he can see more blood. Especially on the kitchen table. "This is we're they took the bullet out. By the looks of all this blood he was hit in his upper left shoulder just missing his heart." Green said. Lieutenant Post immediately got on the radio.

For all officers to check both hospitals. Bridgeport and st. Vincent's. Plus animal hospitals. One of the officers calls out the lieutenant. Both Green and Post follows the police officer to a room on the second floor. That was full of monitors. It shows Green house and the Bridgeport police department. Lieutenant Post immediately called for a search of the police department. Another officer calls for the lieutenant. They followed him to the basement we're they found a Machine some businesses use to make copies of keys. "This is how the got into the police department. Wait till I go to sleep and make copies of my keys." After Green said that he felt like crap. Then in walked captain Martinez.

He pauses for a moment then says. "Change the locks on all doors in the department. Plus the security pass code for the doors and cameras and all evidences." He gave Green a dirty look then walked away. Then another officer came towards Green and Post. "They found Joe Dickerson. He is eating dinner with the Mayor of Bridgeport." Green started to laugh. So did lieutenant Post. "He has the perfect alibi. Nothing we can do can't touch him." Post says. "Unless you find the shooters. Plus, you have his DNA." Green says. "We don't have enough evidence to compel him to give us his DNA." Lieutenant Post says. They began to see at least three police cars driving off immediately. Green and lieutenant Post look to the officer next to them.

He put the cell phone down and speaks. "They found the shooters over at the back entrance of Beardsley Park. Trumball police noticed a car smoking and shot up. Three bodies in the car. Green turns to lieutenant Post. "I'm going to go finish getting my stuff and leave Bridgeport. Have fun there about to be a gang war." Green then leaves finish getting his stuff and drives off. Green walks into the holiday Inn. He notices that it's quiet. He then feels a gun on the back of his head. The the living room lights comes on. Green recognizes the person on the couch. "Sit down detective Green. We need to talk about your family. Don't worry about your daughter she is fine and safe with your sister-in-law.

The commission sent me detective. Remember you owe us. Someone has to answer for all those cops killed at Murphy's Law. We know you have nothing to do with it.

THE END

Made in United States
Orlando, FL
04 July 2024